WHAT GEESE CAN'T FLY?

INSPIRED BY A TRUE STORY

Original Screenplay by
Emily Fagundo Haggman
and Eric Haggman

Story by
Emily Fagundo Haggman
and Joe Fagundo

Trapped between two cultures, a young immigrant girl longs to leave her family's old world ways behind, but fears she is destined to live a life that they have chosen for her.

Review & Praise for 'What Geese Can't Fly'

"*Thoughtfully-crafted and poignant, this beautifully written script is an honest and an often difficult portrayal of what it means to come to America with nothing but hope. Grace's family endures a great deal of hardship. Set within the beautiful, quaint landscape of Cambridge, Massachusetts, their obstacles are jarring. The story excels in painting the picture of wealth disparity in America, Grace's family juxtaposed with the ignorant, elitist mindset of others like Alex.*

Voiceover is effectively used, as well, digging deep and emphasizing the emotions that Grace feels as she attempts to navigate through a tumultuous coming-of-age. She and her family are three-dimensional and fully defined. Each member of the house has his or her own specific obstacles, definitive conflicts. But there's also a strong, overarching family bond that connects them. It helps them survive unspeakable tragedy. The prose is beautiful. It's poetic and rife with emotion.

Characters speak with an authenticity while still retaining an edge that makes the overall story feel cinematic and worthy of the big screen."

–The Black List,
an annual survey of Hollywood executives' favorite unproduced screenplays

This book is a work of fiction. References to real people, events, establishments, organizations, or locales are only intended to provide a sense of authenticity, and are used fictitiously. All other characters, incidents, and dialogue are drawn from the author's imagination and are not to be construed as real.

WHAT GEESE CAN'T FLY?

Copyright © 2020 by Emily Fagundo Haggman

WGAW #1896164

All rights reserved. Printed in the United States of America. No part of this book may be used or reproduced in any manner whatsoever without written permission except in the case of brief quotations embodied in critical articles and reviews.
For more information, email us at emily@haggman.com.

First Edition

Library of Congress Cataloging-in-Publication Data has been applied for.

ISBN 979-8-6210804-8-8 (softcover)

To Mommy and Daddy,

thank you for teaching me how to fly.

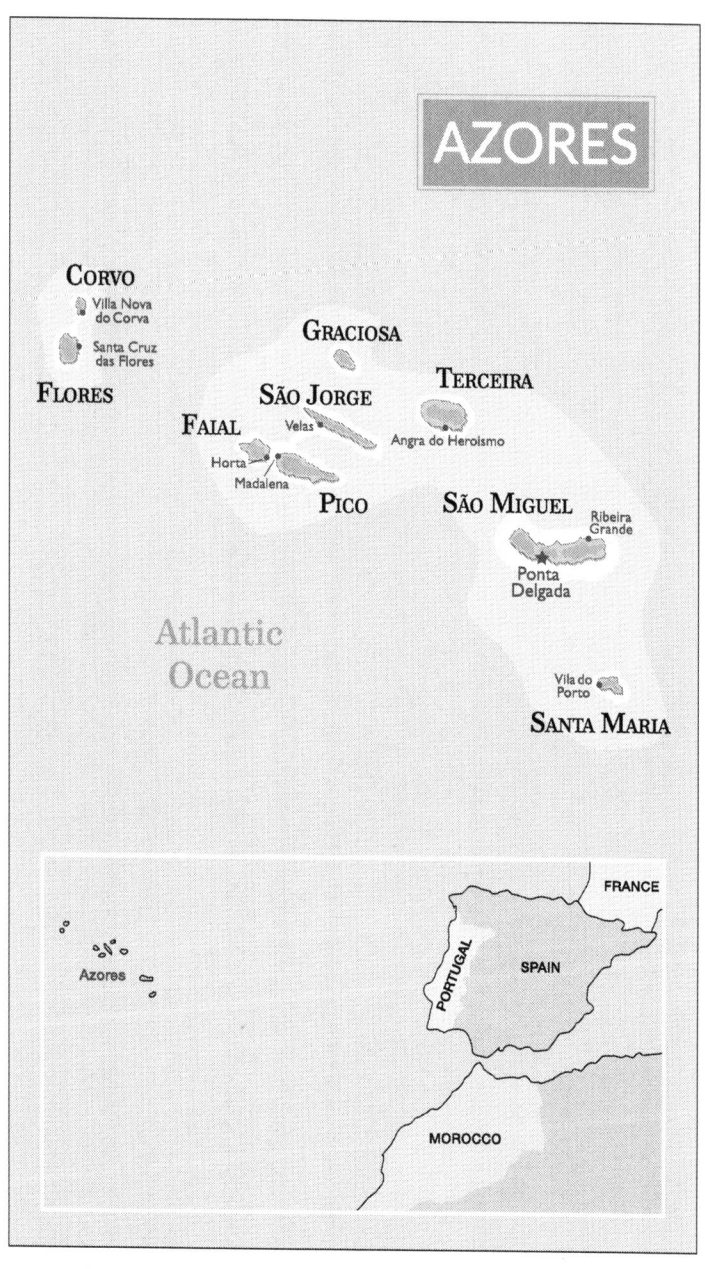

The Azores Islands are a Portuguese archipelago in the North Atlantic Ocean, located about two hours from Europe and five hours from North America.

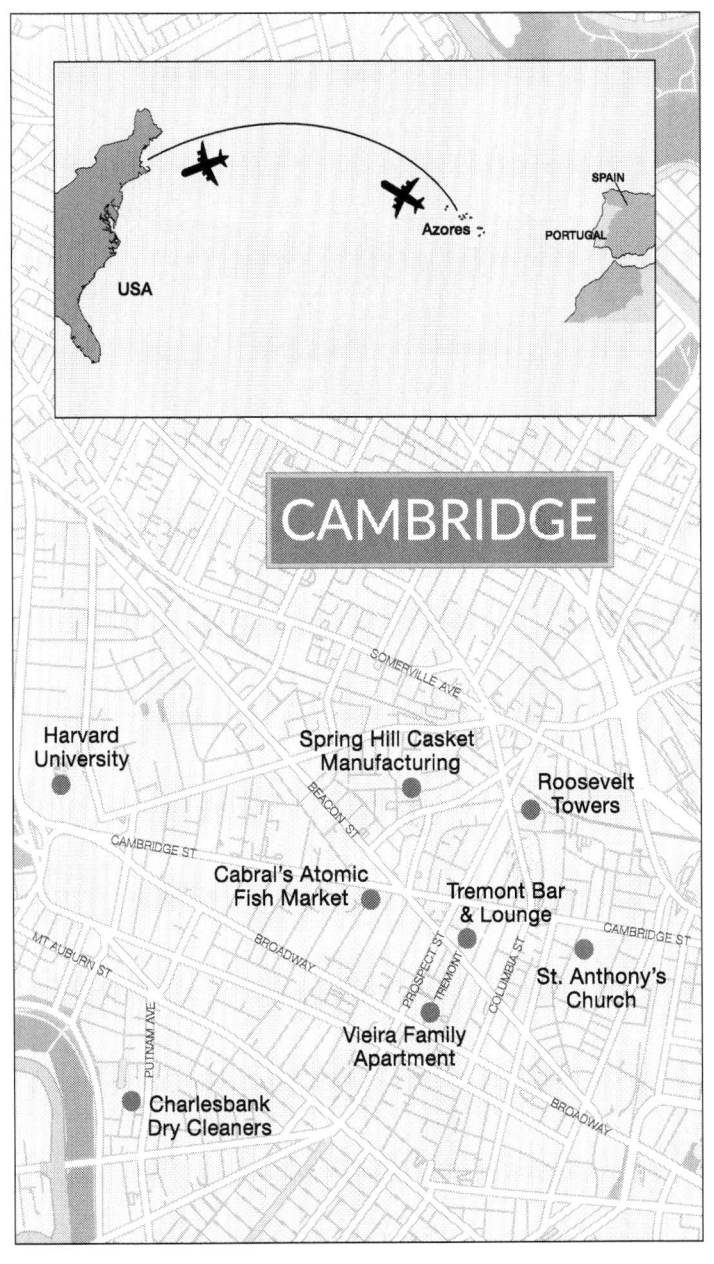

"The People's Republic of Cambridge" - where the story is set and what would become our new home in America.

CAST OF CHARACTERS

Vieira Family
Bella - mother
Fatima - older daughter
Johnny - son
Grace - younger daughter

Fatima's Husband
Eddie Pacheco

Johnny's Posse
Tommy Callahan
Fat Manny
Little Louie

Alex McPhearson
The professor

Joey Medeiros
Grace's boyfriend

Billy Maguire
The bully

Neighborhood Peeps
Turtle
Jimmy O'Leary
Senhora Medeiros

OPENING SCENE

1 EXT. DAY - CAMBRIDGE STREET (MASSACHUSETTS) - SUMMER

LITTLE LISBON: Azores Travel, Manny's Corner Store: tripe & linguica on sale, Maria's Casa de Beauty, Cabral's Atomic Fish Market and triple decker apartments dot the working-class neighborhood.

Juggling a stack of books - a pretty, college age girl breezes through the noisy urban street.

Bronzed olive skin peeks through her yellow sundress as her shiny black hair bounces in sync with her hurried steps.

> GRACE (V.O.):
> *This is my neighborhood ... the People's Republic of Cambridge. Our anchor stores are Cabral's Atomic Fish Market and the Tremont Bar & Lounge.*

Rounding the corner, she SPEEDS up passing the seedy bar and Roosevelt Towers - a dirty, dangerous housing projects.

(Shots of Harvard, wealthy Brattle Street neighborhoods)

> GRACE (V.O.):
> *Around the corner are the Projects, where dreams go to die. And up the street Harvard Square - with its million dollar homes and trust fund babies whose dreams never seem to die.*

About to cross the street, a shiny black Porsche speeds through a red light BLOCKING the four-way intersection. A Toyota Prius, with a "Save the Bees" bumper sticker, SCREECHES to a halt in front of Grace.

> GRACE (V.O.):
> *Dopeheads, rich left-wing liberals and little old ladies dressed in their widow's black living all together in a state of total disdain for one another.*

2 *INT. BLACK PORSCHE*

JOHNNY VIEIRA (30's), presses HARD on his car horn.

We catch a glimpse of his sad, lived-in brown eyes as he covers them with his Ray-Bans.

3 *EXT. CAMBRIDGE STREET*

Raking his hands through his dark, curly hair, Johnny leaps out of the car, rushes towards his self-created gridlock.

SHOUTING at the "bee saving" Prius driver, Johnny abruptly STOPS yelling as he spots GRACE VIEIRA - our narrator - a sweet-faced girl, with laughing eyes and a disarming smile ... (a bright light amidst grim circumstances).

She beams him a sunny smile, waves.

Johnny nods. Turns and darts back inside his Porsche.

4 EXT. SPRING HILL CASKET MANUFACTURING

Grace passes a bunch of Tony Soprano wannabes - young, neighborhood guys hanging outside the casket factory chain smoking, talking shit - as a truck is loaded up with coffins.

> LITTLE LOUIE (pointing over at Grace, wolf-whistling):
> *Look at the knockers on that one.*

Grace totally ignores the comment as Little Louie continues.

> LITTLE LOUIE:
> *Hey baby! Why don't ya come over here and give me some lovin'!*

CLOSE VIEW ON LITTLE LOUIE.

WHACK! His head snaps forward as a beefy hand hits him hard on the back of the head.

> LITTLE LOUIE:
> *Hey! What the ...*

Little Louie turns around as, six-foot-three, three hundred pound, FAT MANNY grabs him by the scruff of the neck.

> FAT MANNY (blue collar accent):
> *What? Are ya' friggin nuts?*

> LITTLE LOUIE:
> *Come on. It's just some good lookin' broad with big tits.*

> FAT MANNY (dangling Louie by the neck):
> *What? You been livin' in a freakin' cave? You idiot! That's GRACE VIEIRA. AS IN JOHNNY VIEIRA. That's his little sista. If he was here right now, he'd stuff your dumb ass in one of them friggin' coffins.*

5 INT. CHARLESBANK DRY CLEANERS - CONTINUOUS

A conveyor belt packed with plastic-bagged clothing whirs and rotates behind Grace as she waits on customers from behind a counter.

We spot her books tucked in the corner.

Customers walk in and out: pleasant, smiling, polite.

An impeccably dressed, older, Asian man enters carrying his shirts wrapped in newspaper. He bows. Grace bows back, counts his shirts, hands him a ticket.

> GRACE:
> *Doumo Arigatou, Mr. Nakamura.*

Big smile, bows.

> MR. NAKAMURA:
> *You're welcome, Miss Grace-san.*

Mr. Nakamura is followed by a tight-jawed, Boston Brahman. Dressed in Brooks Brothers head to toe, expensive loafers, no socks. Talking on his cell phone, he flings Grace his ticket.

Grace just stands there as he continues talking.

> TIGHT-ASS BRAHMAN:
> *He will never be Club material. We all know if it were not for affirmative...*

(annoyed)

> *What are you waiting for?*

> GRACE:
> *Sorry your clothes aren't back.*

> TIGHT-ASS BRAHMAN (slowly separating his words as if Grace were a dimwit):
> *What? I made it perfectly clear when I dropped it off this morning that I needed my tuxedo for dinner at the Harvard Club tonight.*
>
> GRACE:
> *I'm so sorry Mr. Eliot. We lost power this afternoon and everything's backed up.*
>
> TIGHT-ASS BRAHMAN:
> *That's not my problem.*
>
> GRACE:(sliding back his ticket):
> *Well. It kinda is.*

He crumples the ticket, throws it at Grace. Stomps out.

> TURTLE (chuckling, Portuguese accent):
> *We no lose no power today.*

Behind Grace stands TURTLE - short, round, with his hunched-up, turtle-like shoulders - unsuccessfully trying to tuck his shirttails into his pants.

> GRACE:
> *No, we did not. MR. ONE-PER-CENTER just needed a little life lesson. Every time he comes in here he treats us like the great unwashed.*

Pulling his clean, bagged tux off the conveyor belt, she tears off the ticket, crumples it and NBA-like throws it in the trash bucket.

> GRACE:
> *Think this is going M.I.A. for a while.*

TURTLE (laughing with approval):
Grace, them people. They don't like us. It's just like the old country. The rich people on the mainland, they own the boats. And us. We work their boats. They're all the same.

6 EXT. 1/2 MILE UP ON CAMBRIDGE STREET - CONTINUOUS

Johnny speeds up the street, darting in and out of traffic, arguing on his cell phone.

GRACE (V.O.):
Here's what they don't get about us - living in their fancy Brattle Street houses, listening to NPR. All we want is to just fit in. You know ... Belong.

7 EXT. SPRING HILL CASKETS

Johnny roars up in front as Fat Manny, Little Louie and his "posse" rush up to greet him. Fat Manny reaches over, pulls open Johnny's car door.

FAT MANNY:
Hey Johnny. How's it goin'? Everything's ready for you inside.

CUT TO:

8 GRAPHIC: EARLIER, IN THE AZORES, PORTUGAL - BEFORE COMING TO AMERICA

SUN SETS - bathing the black volcanic cliffs in pink and orange hues; fishing boats bob up and down, the blue Atlantic waters splash the rocky shore.

Portuguese Fado music softly begins ... as the Queen of Fado, Amália Rodrigues, sings in Portuguese "Estranha Forma de Vida" ... "This Strange Life."

> AMALIA (V.O.) (Singing in Portuguese):
> *I live in the sadness of this strange life. This heart of mine beating, longing for lives lost.*

Fado music continues ...

9 INT. AIRPLANE WINDOW - DUSK, RED-ORANGE SUN

The sun streaks the face of pretty, doe-eyed 16-year-old FATIMA VIEIRA. Her mother, BELLA, sits next to her holding a crying baby GRACE. JOHNNY's little boy hand reaches over to comfort the baby, gently patting her back.

Bella hugs Grace in closer, hiding her tear-stained face into the tucks of the baby's blanket.

Weeping, Fatima palms the window as an aerial view of the Azores, Portugal passes below.

Fado Music continues ...

10 EXT. SAN MIGUEL, AZORES, PORTUGAL - DUSK

A blaze of purple hydrangeas ZOOMS by as the plane gains altitude.

> GRACE (V.O.):
> *The island of San Miguel where generations of my family have lived. The beauty of the island has long been lost on its people. Lost from a sense of fatalism born of isolation.*

As the island darkens, church bells CLANG. A signal for mothers to scoop up playing children from their stoops; for shop owners to close; for fishermen to tie up their boats.

> GRACE (V.O.):
> *Lost from TOTAL domination by the Catholic Church. Lost from decades under a corrupt, brutal dictatorship. Leaving them still with one shared feeling. FEAR.*
>
> *Fear of speaking the truth. Fear of being overheard. Fear of just disappearing in the middle of the night.*

Boom, boom, boom. A flurry of shutters SHUT CLOSE all over the island.

> GRACE (V.O.):
> *All living in a hopeless psychic prison. One my Vieira family longed to leave behind.*

FADO MUSIC FADES.

ACT 1

EARLY YEARS IN AMERICA

11 EXT. CAMBRIDGE STREET, CAMBRIDGE, MA - DAY
JARRING CITY SOUNDS AS ...

TEN-YEAR-OLD JOHNNY VIEIRA crosses the same four-way intersection where we first met him ... arguing with the "Bee Saving" Prius driver.

Johnny rushes past triple decker apartments and shops - in this RUNDOWN working-class neighborhood.

SEQUENCE OF SHOTS: O'Brien's Liquors, Colleen's Cut & Dry, Sam's Deli & Meats ... An elderly woman dressed in black sweeps the sidewalk in front of one tiny, out of place and time Portuguese shop - Cabral's Fish Market.

12 INT. VIERA FAMILY APARTMENT LANDING, CAMBRIDGE

Taking two steps at a time, Johnny climbs up the three flights.

Women ARGUING in Portuguese.

He STOPS. Heads towards a door marked with a wooden crucifix. Hesitantly, puts his ear up against the door - LISTENS.

13 INT. VIEIRA KITCHEN

Dated appliances, faded wallpaper, plastic covered windows, mismatched Salvation Army furniture.

The meager conditions are masked by colorful ethnic touches: bright curtains, plastic flowers and a huge crucifix of Jesus' limp body hanging on the cross.

BELLA VIEIRA - matriarch - strong-boned with kind eyes - wearing a faded house dress, a multi-colored Portuguese scarf tied around her head, a Saint Michael Archangel medallion necklace hangs from around her neck.

FATIMA VIEIRA - the lovely, petite 16 year-old girl we first met on the plane - sits at the table peeling potatoes. Plopping a potato into the bowl of water, it SPLASHES back on her face.

> FATIMA (in Portuguese):
> *I hate it here. I hate this stupid country.*

Bella vigorously stirs a pot on the stove, wipes at her brow.

> BELLA: (in Portuguese)
> *And what Fatima? You think this is the life I wanted?*

> FATIMA (in Portuguese):
> *It was your choice to leave. Not mine. You should've left me behind.*

> BELLA (in Portuguese, defeated):
> *CHOICE? You know we weren't safe there.*

Sobbing, Fatima runs past ONE-YEAR-OLD, BABY GRACE - sitting in her high chair licking a spoon. Bella chases after Fatima.

> BELLA (Portuguese):
> *Fatima ... You saw what those animals did to your father.*

14 INT. VIEIRA KITCHEN - CONTINUOUS

A pot sits bubbling on top of the hot stove. Baby Grace sits in her high chair CRYING.

Johnny swoops in - scooping up Baby Grace in his arms.

> JOHNNY:
> *Oh Grace ... It's okay, Baby Girl.*

Grace squirms - happy, safe in Johnny's arms.

Fatima's SOBS fill the room.

15 INT. BELLA'S SMALL BEDROOM

Bella kneels, praying before a dresser that is littered with religious figures and a framed picture of JOSE, - THE FATHER. A candle flickers next to it.

> BELLA (praying):
> *Ave Maria cheia de graça, Deus ...*

Johnny gently touches Bella's shoulder. Sits Grace on the floor, kneels and prays beside his mother.

FLASHBACK:

16 INT. VIEIRA FAMILY KITCHEN, AZORES, PORTUGAL - DAY

In the kitchen, MUSIC PLAYS from an old record player as JOSE twirls and turns a BEAMING, LAUGHING Bella around ... serenading her.

> GRACE (V.O.):
> *There's a word in Portuguese called 'saudades'... it means 'longing'... longing for something you left behind, but yet, it never leaves you.*

(a beat)

> *Leaving changed my mother - forever.*

17 INT. JOHNNY'S BEDROOM - MORNING

Bella, wearing a drab old coat over her factory work clothes, stands at the doorway steadying GRACE on her hip.

Johnny's asleep in a crammed bedroom with two twin beds and a crib.

> BELLA (in Portuguese):
> *Johnny. Get up. It's time for school.*

> JOHNNY (in Portuguese):
> *I don't wanna go to school.*

> (in English):
> *I hate school.*

> BELLA (in Portuguese, hurried):
> *There's a lot of things I hate too! GET UP!*

Door SLAMS shut.

18 INT. SIXTH GRADE CLASSROOM - DAY

Wearing hand-me-downs, Johnny sits in the back row. His dark, olive features totally out of place among the sea of blue- eyed, blonde-haired, ten-year-olds.

The children eagerly raise their hands as the teacher walks up, down the rows carrying an English Grammar book.

> TEACHER:
> *Melissa.*

Child stands, reads aloud. Teacher calls out names.

> TEACHER:
> *Kelly, Michael, Gloria ...*

Johnny sinks deeper into his seat as teacher gets closer.

> TEACHER:
> *John Vieira, you're next.*

Petrified. His big, brown eyes look like melting Milk Duds.

> TEACHER:
> *Johnny, it's your turn to read.*

Class snickers. Johnny grows red with embarrassment.

> TEACHER: (impatient, taps on desk):
> *Come on Johnny. Everyone has to participate in my classroom.*

Reluctantly, he stands. Stammers and stutters as he reads. EVERYONE STARES. LAUGHS.

In the back row, sits BILLY MAGUIRE - BIG, blonde, tough - born to repeat a grade.

BILLY MAGUIRE (bellows):
Dumb Port-A-Gee can't even read. Why don't you go back to where you came from.

Class laughs louder. The teacher RAPS on the desk.

TEACHER:
Billy Maguire, that's enough. Johnny, sit down.

Humiliated, swallowing back tears and hate, Johnny sinks down low in his seat.

19 INT. CAMBRIDGE #91 BUS - CONTINUOUS

Dressed in a new bus driver uniform, EDDIE PACHECO (mid 20's), greets passengers with pride - like he's the CAPTAIN of the QE2. His good looks, perfectly coifed pompadour set him apart from the working-class passengers.

EDDIE (Boston accent):
Mornin' Mrs. O'Brien. Mr. O'Toole. Mr. Garcia, how's the leg?

Nods and smiles as they drop money into the fare box.

A frazzled Bella enters. She's balancing a CRYING Grace on one hip and a grocery bag on the other. She struggles to find the change in her pocket.

Eddie covers the fare box with his hand and waves her on.

20 EXT. OUTSIDE SCHOOL YARD - LATER THAT AFTERNOON

School bell RINGS.

Droves of kids rush out, banding together in cliques. Johnny walks out, ALONE. Big Billy Maguire lurks at the end of the courtyard, sneaking cigarettes with his buddies.

> BILLY MAGUIRE (pointing at Johnny):
> *There he is.*

They hop on their bikes. Rush towards Johnny - circling him like shark bait.

> BILLY MAGUIRE (taunting, mimicking Johnny's stutter):
> *Hey J-J-J-Johnny, what kinda geese can't fly?*
> *J-J-J-Johnny? What kinda geese can't fly?*

(laughing wildly)

> *Port-a-Geese, dumb Port-a-Geese. JUST like you,*
> *J-J-J Johnny.*

Johnny stands. Fists clenched, staring Billy down - refusing to show fear.

Billy pulls at Johnny's old jacket.

> BILLY MAGUIRE:
> *Hey J-J-J-Johnny. Where'd you get that jacket?*

> JOHNNY (stuttering):
> *M-M-M-My mother.*

> BILLY MAGUIRE (mean spirited):
> *Oh yeah, she been barrel picking again.*

They circle closer and closer.

Johnny, fighting back tears, makes a run for it.

On the other side of the street is an old cemetery. He dashes across ... disappearing into it.

21 EXT. CEMETERY

Weeds strangle decaying headstones etched with Irish and old Boston Brahman names; Dennis Thomas Riley, Mary Elizabeth Trowbridge ...

Johnny steps over vodka and rum nips. Finds a sunny spot. Sticks his hand in his pocket and pulls out two green plastic Army men. Lays then down on the ground, plays.

A large shadow hovers over him.

Johnny stops playing. CLOSE UP ON JOHNNY'S FACE:

OH SHIT moment ... no way he's turning around.

> TOMMY CALLAHAN:
> *Hey kid.*

Not moving, swallowing hard ... Johnny cranes his neck.

Towering over him is tall, thin TOMMY CALLAHAN (16) wearing a red bandana over his long stringy hair and three-hundred pound Fat Manny (17). EYES GLASSY. BLOODSHOT.

> TOMMY CALLAHAN:
> *Why ain't you in school?*

Johnny EYES Tommy.

> JOHNNY:
> *I hate school.*

> FAT MANNY:
> *Oh yeah, who don't?*

Tommy takes a long drag on a joint.

> TOMMY CALLAHAN:
> *What's your name?*

JOHNNY (slowly):
JJJohnny. Johnny Vieira.

TOMMY CALLAHAN (pointing to himself):
Tommy Callahan ...

(then to Manny)

This here is Fat Manny.

Listen to me, Johnny Vieira ... School sucks. It's a GAME for LOSERS.

Tommy digs into his jacket pocket. Pulls out a bag of marijuana. Wiggles it ...

TOMMY CALLAHAN:
Come on.

Confused, Johnny shrugs.

Tommy extends him a hand up, he takes it. Tommy wraps his arm around Johnny's shoulder.

TOMMY CALLAHAN:
Let's go get high little man.

22 INT. MARKET BASKET GROCERY STORE - LATER LONG SHOT OF THE SNACK FOOD AISLE

Johnny's sitting in a wheelchair, a blanket covers his legs. The chair's marked "Property of Cambridge Hospital." Playing along, Johnny's head bends to his left: sad, pathetic.

HUMMING, Tommy wheels Johnny down the aisle, casually stealing junk food as Johnny tucks it under the blanket.

People pass, and look at little Johnny with pity.

23 *INT. HOTEL SONESTA, CAMBRIDGE, GUEST ROOM*

Dressed in a pink hotel maid uniform, Fatima fluffs a pillow on a guest bed. She SINGS a religious song in Portuguese.

> GRACE (V.O.):
> *Fatima was the prettiest girl on the island. Father Garcia even picked her to be the Virgin Mary in the church's Nativity play. That's like being canonized for a month.*
>
> FATIMA (singing in Portuguese):
> *Quão Grande é o meu Deus ...*

Dressed in his bus driver uniform, a grinning Eddie FRAMES the entrance of the door with his height.

Fatima's long, black ponytail swings with her every move as she pulls up the comforter ... SINGING.

Eddie JINGLES the big ring of keys hanging from his belt.

> EDDIE:
> *You sound pretty.*
>
> FATIMA (startled, broken English):
> *Ai meu Deus, Eddie. You scare me.*
>
> EDDIE:
> *Sorry baby. Just checkin' in on my girl.*

He playfully tugs her ponytail, draping it around her neck then gently kisses her forehead. She's dwarfed by his height.

> EDDIE:
> *You are way too beautiful Fatima to be cleaning other people's toilets.*

Sliding her hands into her uniform's pockets, Fatima smiles shyly.

Eddie leaps backwards and flops onto the newly made bed. He PATS the spot next to him.

> FATIMA:
> *Eddie, I just make that.*

Eddie leans back, cradling his arms behind his head.

> EDDIE:
> *Maybe it's time you stopped making other people's beds.*

(tapping the wad of keys)

> *You know. I got me a good job. Maybe. Maybe it's time we get married.*

> FATIMA:
> *Marries? Reallies?*

> EDDIE (laughing):
> *Reallies.*

Eddie grabs for her hand and pulls her onto the bed as she falls towards him giggling.

CUT TO:

24 INT. TOMMY'S VOLKSWAGEN VAN - NIGHT

An old mattress lines the back of the van. It's jam-packed with goods - from junk food, to shoe laces, to rolls of ribbon - a crammed Dollar Store.

The van is filled with smoke.

Tommy is driving, smoking a joint, singing off key to The Rolling Stones on the radio.

> TOMMY CALLAHAN (singing):
> *Timmmmmmmme is on my side. Oh Yes it is...*

Fat Manny pounds Devil Dogs into his mouth, eating them in one bite.

25 EXT. OUTSIDE OF JOHNNY'S TRIPLE DECKER

The triple decker is pitch black, except for one window.

Tommy's van pulls up - the radio BLARING.

An old lady PEEKS out through the window blinds. The passenger side door opens. Johnny gets in.

26 EXT. TRAIN TRACKS OUTSIDE DEPARTMENT STORE

The tracks are lined with freight trains.

Tommy and Fat Manny are dressed in dark camouflage clothes, black grease paint covering their faces - over the top.

Tommy has a cigarette in one hand, a pair of wire cutters in the other. Fat Manny swings a flashlight.

> TOMMY CALLAHAN:
> *I got this one from a buddy of mine. He works the night shift. There's trains here with cigarettes... Think of the money we'll make selling 'em.*

> JOHNNY (clocking the miles of trains):
> *What train is it?*

> TOMMY CALLAHAN:
> *I don't know. It's not like he told me everything.*

Walking up and down the tracks, circling the trains, Tommy starts to sniff around, smelling for tobacco.

> TOMMY CALLAHAN:
> *Come on help me out here. Take a whiff. Maybe we can smell 'em out.*

Johnny SHOOTS him a WTF look but joins in the "smell fest" anyway. Fat Manny gets closer to Tommy. SNIFFS.

> TOMMY CALLAHAN:
> *What? You find something?*
>
> FAT MANNY:
> *Yeah. I smell dog shit.*

Tommy's stepped in a big pile of dog shit. He starts scraping his sneakers against the train track.

> TOMMY CALLAHAN (looking down):
> *Oh man, I just stole these bad boys yesterday.*

Johnny's hysterically laughing.

> TOMMY CALLAHAN:
> *Shhh! Shhh! Did you hear that?*

Johnny shakes his head, no.

> TOMMY CALLAHAN:
> *Listen.*

They all stand completely still, listening.

VOICES talking in the distance ... getting closer.

> TOMMY CALLAHAN (pointing to a train):
> *Come on. Quick, let's try this one.*

Tommy cuts the lock off the train's door.

Jumps inside: Dozens of long cardboard boxes fill the cabin of the train.

> TOMMY CALLAHAN (elated):
> *This is it. This is it! Oh my God! We're gonna be loaded.*

Tommy pulls out a knife. SLASH. Slices open the boxes.

CLOSE VIEW ON A DUMBFOUNDED TOMMY.

> TOMMY CALLAHAN:
> *BROOOOOMS??? What THE FUCK are we gonna do with brooms?*

CUT TO:

27 INT. VIEIRA TRIPLE DECKER - DAY

Looking so pretty in a powder blue summer dress, Fatima has Johnny by the hand, pulling him towards a Chevy Impala.

> JOHNNY:
> *Stop dragging me. Where are we going?*

> FATIMA:
> *To the carnival. Mama say I can go with Eddie if you come with me.*

Johnny lags behind as Fatima drags him towards the Impala - where Eddie sits behind the wheel ... admiring himself in the mirror.

28 EXT. SAUGUS ELKS CLUB CARNIVAL

The large makeshift carnival is set up in an open parking lot across from the Squires Strip Club. A multi-colored Ferris wheel dots the background, Carnival Barkers, YELLING, selling their games and fried dough.

> CARNIVAL BARKER (standing next to The High Striker game):
> *Test ya' strength here. Are you Olive Oyl or Popeye? Come on over. Test ya' strength.*

SEQUENCE OF SHOTS: Eddie and Fatima - holding hands, eating cotton candy.

Eddie shows Johnny how to shoot a basketball into the Hoop of Tower game. Winning. Choosing a prize.

29 *INT. EDDIE'S CHEVY IMPALA*

Johnny sits in the backseat trying to spin his newly won basketball on his finger. Towering next to him is a huge black and white stuffed panda bear.

Under Eddie's driver's seat rests a six pack of beer.

Eddie holds a can in one hand, the other is wrapped around Fatima as he steers the car with his knee. He offers Fatima a sip.

> FATIMA:
> *No Eddie. I no drink.*
>
> EDDIE:
> *I like that. Good girls don't drink.*

They roll up in front of Fatima's triple decker. Eddie parks, turns around towards Johnny, who's sleeping against the stuffed panda.

> EDDIE (shaking Johnny awake):
> *Hey! Snooze on your own time.*

30 *EXT. OUTSIDE EDDIE'S CAR*

Johnny gets out, cradling his new basketball and dragging the ginormous panda by its ear.

EDDIE (yelling out):
Make sure you give that bear to your baby sista. Now, get lost.

31 INT. EDDIE'S CAR

Eddie grabs another beer and pulls Fatima closer to him, feeling the effects of the beer.

EDDIE:
You think your Ma is ever gonna let us go out on a date alone?

FATIMA (shaking her head):
No Eddie. She no likes. Is okay when we marries.

EDDIE (a bit aggressive):
Come on, that's bullshit. This ain't the old country. It's freakin' America.

Eddie guzzles the beer. CRUSHES the can and lobs it into the back seat. It rolls off, CLINKS onto the aluminum graveyard of crushed beer cans littering the floor board.

CUT TO:

32 INT. TOMMY'S VAN - NEXT DAY

Sitting in the back of his van, Tommy's drinking beer and smoking dope as he musses up Johnny's hair — smearing what looks like dirt on his face.

Tommy passes Johnny the joint. He takes an inexperienced drag on the joint - CHOKES and COUGHS.

33 *EXT. TOMMY'S VAN IN FRONT OF A LARGE SUBURBAN HOUSE*

Johnny's standing outside the van. Waif-like. His hair is messed up, face smudged - looking like Oliver Twist.

He's carrying a new broom. But the broom is elaborately decorated with colorful ribbons.

Johnny reluctantly trudges towards the house, Tommy, cupping his hands, YELLS out from the van.

> TOMMY CALLAHAN (slowly separating his words):
> *Don't forget the line about your BLIND father.*

Johnny rings the doorbell.

A nicely dressed woman answers. Johnny hands her the broom, selling his story. She ruffles his hair. Pulls out some dollar bills from her apron pocket.

CLOSE UP VIEW ON JOHNNY, TURNING TOWARDS TOMMY - SMILING.

34 *INT. VIEIRA KITCHEN - NEXT MORNING*

Johnny, wearing his little boy underwear, spots a bowl of Froot Loops cereal on the table. He munches on a handful, walks towards the fridge, grabs the milk.

A cat PURRS.

Looking down, he pets the cat. Shakes the milk carton. Picks up his cereal bowl, dumps it out. Pours the milk into the bowl, gives it to the cat.

35 INT. HALLWAY

Johnny, still in his underwear, sits on the floor playing with a bucket of green, plastic Army soldiers.

The front door OPENS.

Johnny perks up, LISTENS.

36 INT. APARTMENT DOOR

Fatima's wearing her pink hotel maid's uniform.

> FATIMA:
> *Come. Come Eddie. Nobody home.*

Eddie, dressed in his bus driver uniform, drinking a beer follows with his big wad of keys dangling from his belt.

37 INT. HALLWAY

Johnny leans flat up against the wall. Listens.

38 INT. KITCHEN

Fatima and Eddie flirt, he grabs for her, she pulls away.

She strikes a match under the old kettle. Eddie gulps down his beer.

> FATIMA:
> *I make you some thing to eat.*

He reaches for her butt, but she fends him off.

> FATIMA:
> *Eddie, come, you sit down.*

She pulls cheese and butter out of the fridge.

Eyes downcast, she uncovers the bread that's on the table.

Eddie - oblivious to her mood - paws at her while simultaneously putting a big hunk of cheese in his mouth.

> EDDIE:
> *Come here baby. Come sit on Big Daddy's lap.*

(He pats his thigh and looks down at his crotch.)

> *Big Eddie wants to talk to you.*

With her back to Eddie, Fatima stands by the stove fidgeting with the kettle.

> FATIMA (blurts out):
> *Eddie, I gonna have a baby.*

He chokes on the chunk of cheese - coughing, rambling...

> EDDIE:
> *What? No way. You can't be. I always pulled out in time.*

The kettle WHISTLES.

Eddie gets up. PACES around the kitchen.

> *Okay. Okay, I know. I know this guy. He can make the whole thing disappear.*

(snapping his fingers)

> *Just like that.*

> FATIMA:
> *What you mean?*

EDDIE:
We're gonna get rid of it.

FATIMA:
I no understand.

EDDIE:
I'm gonna get you an abortion.

(slowly, in Portuguese)

A-bor-tamento. No one will ever know.

FATIMA (horrified):
No, Eddie. God, he know everything. Is a bad sin.

EDDIE:
Oh, yeah - but sleeping around ain't a sin?

FATIMA:
You say you love me. We get married.

EDDIE:
Married? Come on, I'm not even sure the kid's mine.

FATIMA (crying):
No Eddie. I never be with nobody's. Only you.

Eddie pulls her in closer to him.

EDDIE:
I know, you're my little Portagee Virgin Mary ...
Come on, there's nothing to worry about. I'll take care
of everything. Trust me, not even God will know.

Fatima REELS at Eddie in rage and starts hitting him.

FATIMA:
NO. No. NO. You lie to me.

Eddie GRABS her by her tiny wrists, pins her up against the wall. She fights back. Tearing the buttons off of his uniform shirt, yanking off his gold cross.

> EDDIE (looking down at his shirt):
> *You little bitch, don't you ever...*

> JOHNNY (yelling, from the doorway):
> *S-S-STOP! STOP hitting my sister.*

STARTLED - they both stop, FROZEN.

CLOSE UP VIEW ON JOHNNY IN THE DOORWAY.

> JOHNNY:
> *Stop hurting her!*

Eddie taunts Johnny - lightly slapping Fatima's face.

> EDDIE:
> *Oh yeah, tough guy. What are you gonna do about it?*

> JOHNNY (stuttering):
> *L-L-Leave her alone.*

Eddie grabs Fatima by the hair, pulling it.

> EDDIE (mimicking):
> *Oh yeah. M-M-M-Make me!*

Johnny grabs the knife off the table. LUNGES for Eddie.

With one hand, Eddie grabs Johnny, knocks him to his butt. The knife falls. Eddie grabs it. Grabs Johnny. Brings the knife up close to his ear.

> EDDIE:
> *You little shithead. I should just cut your ear off.*
> *This ain't none of your business.*

FATIMA:
Eddie no. Please. No hurt him.

Eddie gives Johnny a hard shove against the wall. Grabs for Fatima's arm - she recoils.

EDDIE:
I was never gonna hurt him. You know me, I just wanted to scare the piss out of him.

(puts his arm around Fatima)

Come on baby. You know I love you. Give Eddie a little kiss.

Fatima, fighting back tears, looks away — not wanting to face Johnny.

39 INT. VIEIRA FAMILY KITCHEN, LATER THAT NIGHT

SILENCE ... except for the heavy kneading of dough.

Swallowing back sobs, Fatima stands at the sink washing dishes.

Bella AGGRESSIVELY POUNDS the dough on the counter.

FATIMA (in Portuguese, her head cast down):
He won't marry me.

BELLA (in Portuguese):
Why not?

FATIMA (in Portuguese):
He says the baby isn't his.

BELLA (in Portuguese):
Is it?

Fatima throws the sponge into the sink ... back splashing herself.

> FATIMA (Portuguese):
> *Mama, eu não sou uma PUTA!*
>
> (English)
> *I'm a good girl.*

Bella POUNDS the dough with her fists.

CUT TO:

40 EXT. OUTSIDE A DARK APARTMENT DOOR - DAWN, NEXT DAY

CLOSE VIEW: A woman's big, meaty fist pounds on a door, banging loudly.

> EDDIE:
> *Go away. It's five o'clock in the friggin' morning.*

41 INT. EDDIE'S APARTMENT

KNOCKING continues.

Cheap furniture, beer cans and clothes strewn all about, EXCEPT FOR: his bus driver uniform which is hung neatly over a chair, next to his large wad of bus keys.

In his underwear, wearing his gold cross, a disheveled Eddie heads towards the door.

KNOCKING GROWS LOUDER.

> EDDIE:
> *Hold your fuckin' horses!*

PISSED OFF, he swings open the door.

> EDDIE:
> *This better be good.*

A stern-faced, chubby, older woman, dressed in black from head to toe, stands before him.

> EDDIE:
> *Ma? What are you doing here?*

ANNA PACHECO reaches up and slaps his face. HARD.

Anna barges in, pushing Eddie aside. She's followed in by Bella and Fatima.

42 INT. VIEIRA KITCHEN - ONE WEEK LATER

A morose Eddie stands by the sink tugging on his new wedding ring - sliding it on and off his finger.

Baby Grace sits in a highchair crushing Cheerios on the table with her chubby hands.

Next to her, Johnny and Fatima lean in closer to the radio ... listening to a soccer game.

> PORTUGUESE RADIO ANNOUNCER (exuberant in Portuguese):
> *GOOOOAAAALLLL! GOOOOAAAALLLL!*

RAPPING on the table, Fatima celebrates the goal.

Johnny scoops up Grace, TWIRLING her around the room. LAUGHING.

> GRACE (V.O.):
> *There were pockets of happiness. But they were fleeting. Like there was a hole in your pocket, where the lucky penny kept slipping out.*

> FATIMA (to Johnny):
> *Maybe one day you play futebol. Like papa teach you.*

Johnny smiles, sits Grace back in the highchair ... feeding her a Cheerio.

> EDDIE:
> *So Johnny boy, how's school goin'?*

> JOHNNY (shrugging):
> *I dunno.*

> EDDIE:
> *That's just great. The family brain trust here spends all day in school*

(mocking)

> *learning ... I dunno!*

Eddie pulls a folded letter out of his pocket, flattens it on the table.

> EDDIE (sliding the letter towards Johhny):
> *Maybe this is why.*

Close-up on letter: JOHN VIEIRA TRUANCY WARNING ...Violation of the compulsory attendance can result in referral for court proceedings ...

> EDDIE:
> *They can deport your dumb Portagee ass if you keep on skipping school.*

SMACK! Johnny POUNDS the table with his fists, startling Grace. She CRIES.

> JOHNNY:
> *I hate you Eddie. I don't care what they do. I ain't ever goin' back.*

43 EXT. SCHOOL BUS STOP - NEXT MORNING

Sulking, Johnny is kicking a beer can against the curb.

> JOHNNY:
> *I hate school.*

Wearing a red, white and blue bandana, Tommy's leaning against the fire hydrant, smoking a cigarette.

> TOMMY CALLAHAN:
> *School blows, man. Sucks you got caught.*

Johnny sits down on the curb, crushing the can with his foot.

> JOHNNY:
> *Everybody hates me.*

A bus pulls up filled with kids. Windows open, heads hanging out, kids laughing, shouting.

Billy Maguire sticks his head out the window and tosses his pencil at Johnny's feet.

> BILLY MAGUIRE:
> *Hey, hey Johnny get me my pencil? I dropped it.*

Johnny shakes his head, no.

> BILLY MAGUIRE (pleading):
> *Ah come on, be a pal. It's the only one I got.*

Johnny picks up the pencil and walks toward the bus.

Billy SPITS at him. His buddies ROAR with laughter.

Fists clenched, Johnny stands frozen in rage.

Tommy WHIPS his cigarette at the bus.

He HUCKS up a big glob of spit and aims it directly at Billy - the glob SPLATTERS against the bus window.

> TOMMY CALLAHAN (grabbing Johnny by the shoulders):
> *What the fuck's wrong with you, man. You can't let them mess with you like that. You gotta stand up to those assholes.*

LAUGHING, Billy's buddies PELLET Johnny with their pencils.

> TOMMY CALLAHAN (grabbing Johnny):
> *Come on, come with me.*

Boarding the bus, they MARCH towards Billy Maguire.

Tommy EYES Billy, getting in his face.

> TOMMY CALLAHAN:
> *Hey, you. Asshole. You see this kid.*

(points to Johnny)

> *This is my buddy. AND if you ever, EVER, spit at him again, I'm gonna yank out your friggin' tongue out of your ugly-ass mouth.*

(pokes Billy's chest hard)

> *You GOT that?*

Eyes bulging out of their sockets, Billy nods yes.

Tommy and Johnny walk to the last row and sit.

> TOMMY CALLAHAN:
> *Johnny, listen to me little man. You gotta seriously beat the crap out of that asshole. Really, really hurt him.*

(pause)

> *Oh yeah. One more thing.*
>
> *Make sure someone SEES you do it.*

Johnny's not quite getting it?

> TOMMY CALLAHAN (leaning in closer):
> *So the WORD gets around.*

44 INT. SCHOOL GYMNASIUM, GYM CLASS - DAY

The boys' sixth grade class PLAYS dodge ball. Teams are lined up - throwing the ball at each other. Billy Maguire is fiercely dominating the game.

Billy's aiming for the small, fat boys and Johnny. He aims for Johnny. Misses.

You hear the SMASHING BLOWS as kids get hit. The teacher sits in the bleachers, reading from a clipboard.

> TEACHER (barely interested):
> *You're out. Next up.*

Johnny's up.

Takes his time as he EYES Billy Maguire. Aims. Hits him HARD - taking Billy's breath away.

> BILLY MAGUIRE (pointing at Johnny):
> *You're gonna pay for that.*
>
> TEACHER:
> *Maguire. You're out. Sit down.*

Game continues as Billy GLARES at Johnny.

45 INT. VIEIRA TRIPLE DECKER LANDING - LATER

Johnny enters the front door. From behind, he's punched in the head. BAM! BAM! As Billy and his buddy punch and kick him.

> BILLY MAGUIRE:
> *You dirty, little Port-a-Gee. Thought you were a tough guy, huh?*

Mrs. CABRAL walks out on the landing waving her new broom.

> MRS. CABRAL (yelling):
> *Go away. GET OUT. I call police.*

The boys stop, run out the door - leaving Johnny bruised and bloodied on the floor.

46 INT. BELLA'S BEDROOM - LATER THAT NIGHT

Johnny's curled up on the bed crying. Bella's sitting on the edge holding an ice wrapped towel - gently pressing it against his bruised and swollen face.

A lit candle illuminates Johnny's father's photo on the dresser. Jose's photo slowly MORPHS...

FLASHBACK:

47 INT. TINY VIEIRA KITCHEN - AZORES, NIGHT

TO JOSE VIEIRA's image in the mirror, knotting the tie on his policeman's uniform shirt. He kisses the Saint Michael Archangel medallion hanging from his neck - his protector against the forces of evil.

Bella sits across from him at the kitchen table feeding a squealing baby Grace in her high chair.

BELLA (to Jose in Portuguese):
You should just look the other way Jose. Say nothing. Carlos was born a thief. He's been stealing since he was a little kid.

JOSE (in Portuguese):
Yeah Bella, but it's not just candy he's stealing anymore. Carlos Teixeira's become a very dangerous man. And I know who he's stealing for.

BELLA (in Portuguese):
And that's exactly why you should stay quiet.

Jose gently pinches Grace's chubby cheeks. Kisses Bella on the forehead.

JOSE (to Bella in Portuguese):
You worry too much, meu amor.

Jose grabs his police cap off the table, opens the kitchen door onto the street.

Right as he opens the door: BANG! BANG! BANG! Blood SPRAYS the room, SPLATTERING Bella and Grace in Jose's blood.

CUT BACK TO:

48 *INT. BELLA'S BEDROOM*

BELLA (to Johnny in Portuguese):
Your father died because he had the courage to stand up to some very bad men.

Dropping the towel and cupping Johnny's face in her hands.

BELLA (in Portuguese):
Johnny, your father spoke out when others cowered in fear. He would want you to stand up for yourself and fight back.

CUT TO:

49 *EXT. SCHOOL YARD - DAYS LATER*

Kids are running around. Playing tag, shooting hoops.

In the corner, Billy Maguire and his buddy are spray painting "PORTAGEES SUCK!" on the school wall.

BAM! BAM! BAM! From behind.

Each boy falls to the ground as Johnny whacks them HARD with a broken-off broom stick.

DISSOLVE TO:

Portuguese Fado music softly returns.

ACT 2

50 INT. NEW VIEIRA APARTMENT - TEN YEARS LATER

CLOSE VIEW ON NOW TEN-YEAR-OLD GRACE: TWIRLING around the room, wearing a long, blue satin robe, tied with a gold sash. From under her robe, spring feathered angel wings.

> GRACE (V.O.):
> *Being an angel in the church parade is a Portuguese girl's rite of passage. Your little hands squeezed together in prayer, dutifully walking behind a floating Holy Spirit statue wearing its crown of thorns ... dodging and weaving as the Priest swings the holy incense holder ... trying not to choke on the fumes.*

As cherub-faced Grace spins, the modest, new apartment is revealed: Decorated Portuguese style — gold crushed velvet wall paper, plastic covered sofas, fake flowers, saints galore.

Slowly, three framed pictures appear on the wall: Jesus Christ on the Cross, JOSE - the father, and SPORTEM - the Portuguese soccer team.

FATIMA (slight Portuguese accent):
Hey, Grace. Slow it down.

Grace with her eyes closed, arms spread wide open continues to spin, bumping into a very PREGNANT Fatima.

FATIMA:
Ai' corisca, take it easy. Don't go messin' up your costume before the feast.

GRACE:
I'm practicing my angel flying.

FATIMA:
Great. Then try flyin' to the kitchen, it's time to eat.

51 INT. KITCHEN - DAY

Flowered, fuzzy-balled fringe curtains hang from the windows. Plastic fruit decorations everywhere. A clock featuring The Last Supper TICK TOCKS on the wall.

Bella sets the table with platters of traditional food: codfish, octopus, sardines, huge loaves of bread.

LOUD chatter from the other room - all in ENGLISH.

BELLA (broken English):
Come. Come eats. Venha comer.

Eddie enters wearing a super-sized gold cross and the same pompadour hairstyle from ten years ago. Followed by Fatima, holding the hand of her toddler, Linda.

Tall, strong, fit, sporting a crew cut and wearing a khaki Army uniform - Johnny enters. Bella grabs his face. Kisses him on his forehead, eyes, cheeks...

> BELLA (broken English):
> *Ah Meu Deus. Meu Johnny. So good you home. Your Papa.*

(blesses herself)

> *He be so proud.*

52 INT. HALLWAY

Grace flits down the narrow hallway towards the kitchen. The edges of her angel wings brushing up against the saint-lined wall.

Her moment to SHINE.

About to enter the kitchen, Grace's angel wings get stuck in the doorway. She PUSHES herself through ... no luck.

Laughter ERUPTS, louder and louder the more she attempts.

Eddie SLAPS the table in hysterics.

53 INT. BELLA'S SEWING ROOM, OFF THE HALLWAY - CONTINUOUS

Grace's little sobs fill the hallway.

Johnny pulls back the flowered curtain serving as a door, revealing an old Singer sewing machine, and a small daybed shoved in the corner.

Grace's sitting on the daybed crying. Her little feet dangling.

> GRACE:
> *I'm a stupid angel.*

He kisses her head and looks her straight in the eye.

JOHNNY:
You're the smartest angel in this whole family. Don't you ever forget that.

He gently pulls the little, blue satin robe up over her head. Kneels down on one knee and unhooks the angel wing harness. Pulls the robe back down and grabs her hand.

54 INT. KITCHEN

Holding Johnny's hand, Grace shyly walks into the kitchen.

EDDIE (sarcastically, pointing):
Hey! Houdini. That was some stunt. Next time, why not try flyin' in!

He laughs hysterically at his own stupid joke. Fatima shoots him a long, dirty look - pushing away her plate.

JOHNNY:
You are such an ass, Eddie. Nothing ever changes with you.

EDDIE:
What? Come on. I was making a joke.

FATIMA:
Nobody's laughing Eddie.

BOOM! In a burst of anger, Eddie rises. Kicks over the chair.

EDDIE:
This fuckin' family. You got no goddamn sense of humor.

55 EXT. SAINT ANTHONY'S CHURCH FEAST - DUSK

"The Feast of the Holy Spirit" banner hangs from the church, in Portuguese and English.

Music plays; costumed dancers dance; people eat and drink; kids enjoy the makeshift carnival.

Johnny's surrounded by his 'Portuguese Posse' - the same guys we first met in front of Spring Hill Caskets. Everyone's drinking beers, smoking cigarettes, talking trash.

> FAT MANNY (to Johnny):
> *You was friggin' nuts for volunteerin.' No way I'm gonna go fight nobody I know nothin' about.*
>
> *There's no fuckin' way I'm gettin' my ass blowed up for some foreigners. Let 'em fight their own friggin' battles.*
>
> LITTLE LOUIE:
> *Yeah that's right. And with your big, fat ass - they couldn't miss.*

The guys laugh, jostling each other.

Grace, Fatima and her little girl are riding on the Merry-Go-Round. Fatima holds onto the toddler as they go round and round - laughing.

Across the way, Eddie, his buddies and his cousin, MARIO are yucking it up. Drinking, smoking, checking out women.

> EDDIE (downing his beer):
> *Look at the tits on that one. You could suck on them babies for days.*

Laughter erupts as they further ogle the young woman. Fatima glances over disapproving. Mario catches her eye.

Embarrassed, he waves over. She nods back.

Catching their interaction, Eddie STOMPS his cigarette out on the ground with his foot.

MARIO FURTADO (pointing over):
Hey! Ain't that Johnny over there? When'd he get home?

EDDIE (uninterested):
Yesterday. He just got back.

MARIO:
Call him over. I wanna' see him.

Eddie whistles loudly to get Johnny's attention.

EDDIE (shouting):
Hey John, Johnny. Come here.

Johnny looks straight at him. Turns. Walks away.

EDDIE (yelling louder):
Hey. Didn't you hear me calling?

From behind, Eddie GRABS Johnny by the shoulder.

EDDIE:
What? The army make you too good for your family now?

Johnny pulls Eddie's arm off his shoulder.

JOHNNY:
You're NOT my family.

EDDIE:
I'm married to your fuckin' sista. We're family.

Johnny turns to leave.

Eddie pushes him from behind. Johnny turns around, PUNCHES Eddie HARD. Eddie loses balance. Then LUNGES at Johnny.

Johnny and Eddie are seriously fighting, Eddie is on the losing end.

The sounds of the crowd and fighting intensifies.

Fatima pulls her daughter off the Merry-Go-Round, flings her on her hip.

Grace turns towards the noise and RACES towards Johnny.

>GRACE:
>*John! Johnny!*

Fatima runs after her, grabs her by the wrist, pulling her away. Grace resists.

>GRACE:
>*NO. STOP. Let go of me. He's hurting my Johnny.*

56 EXT. FATIMA AND EDDIE'S APARTMENT DOOR - LATER THAT NIGHT

Eddie, drunk, is struggling with the key - clumsily inserting it into the lock.

>EDDIE:
>*I saw the way you looked at Mario.*

>FATIMA:
>*Eddie, shhhhhhhh. It's late.*

>EDDIE:
>*You wanted him ... didn't you.*

>FATIMA:
>*For Christ's sake, Eddie, I'm seven months pregnant. I don't want nobody.*

Opening the door, turning towards Fatima.

>EDDIE:
>*What's that suppose to mean?*

FATIMA:
It means I ain't exactly feelin' so sexy these days.

EDDIE:
So what are you saying? If you wasn't pregnant, you'd be interested?

FATIMA:
NO. That's not what I mean.

Standing in the doorway, BLOCKING her entrance.

EDDIE:
I know exactly what you mean. Once a whore, always a whore.

SLAM! He shuts the door in her face. Fatima softly raps on the door. Looking around, trying not to wake the neighbors.

FATIMA (softly):
Eddie, please...

57 EXT. VIEIRA APARTMENT DOOR - CONTINUOUS

Hair a mess. Holding her shoes in hand, long runs zigzagging her pantyhose, Fatima stands at the front door INCESSANTLY RINGING the doorbell.

FATIMA:
Come on, somebody answer.

JOHNNY (opening the door):
What's the matter?

FATIMA:
My life, that's the matter.

Fatima pushes past him.

FATIMA:
I have to pee so bad.

58 INT. KITCHEN

John turns the burner on under the kettle. Fatima has her head down on the table, hands covering her face.

JOHNNY:
You want some coffee?

FATIMA (SLAMMING the table):
NO! What I want is a new life. I can't stand him anymore.

JOHNNY (slowly):
Fatima, Eddie Pacheco's a piece of shit. You shoulda' left him a long time ago.

FATIMA:
Oh ya, sure ... you know how Ma feels about that. And where am I suppose to go? Live here with her? Go on welfare? NO Way.

(pause)

Anyways, sometimes, he ain't so bad. But I swear to God, tonight, all's I did was say hi to Mario and, boom, he lost it. It's the booze. It always makes him crazy.

John pulls up a chair, sits close, locks eyes with her.

JOHNNY:
Fatima. Listen to me. Ever since I can remember, Eddie Pacheco's been an asshole. With or without booze. He's never gonna change. And being nice sometimes, just ain't good enough.

Bella enters, wearing a nightgown, holding rosary beads. Grace peeks in from behind her.

> BELLA:
> *What's the matter now, Fatima?*
>
> FATIMA:
> *Everything, Ma. Everything's the matter. My life. My marriage.*
>
> BELLA (Portuguese):
> *And whose fault is that, Fatima?*
>
> FATIMA:
> *Ma, I beg you. Don't start with me. I'm sorry I got pregnant. I'm sorry I disappointed you.*
>
> (in Portuguese):
> *Desculpa. Desculpa. Desculpa.*
>
> JOHNNY:
> *Ma, it's not her fault. Eddie's...*

Grace's EYES DART from Bella to John to Fatima arguing.

> BELLA (interrupting):
> *Married people. They fight. This no your business.*
>
> JOHNNY:
> *Ma. Come on. Go back to bed. Leave her alone for God's sake.*

Bella leaving, turns back to Fatima.

> BELLA (sternly in Portuguese):
> *Remember Fatima. All good, God- fearing mothers make sacrifices for their children. You're no different.*

59 INT. LIVING ROOM - NEXT MORNING

A wall filled with family photos and, yes, saints ... lots of saints surround Grace.

Wearing Barbie pajamas, she sits cross-legged in front of the TV - talking into her pink Barbie phone.

> GRACE (V.O.):
> *I learned a lot about how different we were from watching TV. Everybody's not so sad, or mad or yelling at each other all the time. Sometimes, it's okay to just be happy.*

Still in last night's clothes, Fatima stands at the doorway watching Grace.

> GRACE (on her Barbie phone):
> *Yes. Okay, that will be fine.*

> FATIMA:
> *What are you doing?*

> GRACE:
> *Making reservations.*

> FATIMA:
> *Reservations? You goin' somewhere?*

> GRACE (proudly):
> *Yeah, sure. I saw it on TV. You can go anywhere you want.*

Grace hands Fatima the phone.

> GRACE:
> *Here, you try it. Just pick a place.*

Fatima fidgets with the dial on the toy phone.

FATIMA:
Yeah, don't I wish. I'm not goin' anywhere anytime soon.

CAMERA SEES: TV playing in the background as a smiling "All American Family" sits down for a "No Drama" dinner together.

GRACE (V.O.):
I wanted to be more like them. You know, just eating peanut butter and jelly sandwiches and living in a house without saints staring over your shoulder, watching your every move.

Unconsciously stroking the Saint Michael medallion hanging around her neck, Bella stands by the door ... listening to them.

CUT TO:

60 INT. MCI CORRECTIONAL CENTER (LOW SECURITY PRISON) - DAY

Crammed Visitor's Room. Grimy metal tables line the square concrete block.

Visitors sit on worn, plastic orange chairs waiting to see their Cons.

Johnny studies an old poster taped on the wall - JAIL HOUSE VISITOR'S DRESS CODE: Prohibited attire: Clothing that exposes breasts, chest, genitals or buttocks.

Tommy saunters in wearing an orange jumpsuit. Plops into a matching orange chair across from Johnny.

TOMMY CALLAHAN:
When did ya' get home? And what the fuck they feed you in there? You turned into the Jolly Green Giant.

> JOHNNY (shaking his head):
> *Just last week Tommy. You were first on my list, buddy. How's it going?*
>
> TOMMY CALLAHAN:
> *It sucks ass! You can't catch a break in this friggin' place. The Spooks think you're a Spic, the Spics think you're a Honky Fag and the Irish assholes in here, they fuckin' hate everybody.*
>
> JOHNNY:
> *Callahan ... you do know you're Irish. Right?*
>
> TOMMY CALLAHAN:
> *Yeah, yeah. But I'm not like them. You. Me. We're family.*

Johnny shakes his head. Laughs. He hands Tommy a cigarette.

> JOHNNY:
> *You need anything?*

Tommy pulls one from the pack. Takes a long drag.

> TOMMY CALLAHAN:
> *Just be here to pick me up when I get outta this dump next week. I'm gonna need some weed and pussy - real bad.*

61 INT. VIEIRA KITCHEN - AFTERNOON

Johnny is scanning a thin section of the newspaper "Want Ads." READING: "Experience required," "College degree," "Masters level candidates ..."

Glued to the TV, Grace sits next to Johnny.

Bella HOVERS over Johnny.

BELLA:
So, what now? What you gonna do for work?

Johnny circles the "We Don't Want You Ads" with his finger.

JOHNNY:
I don't know, Ma. Don't have a clue.

GRACE:
Maybe you can go work in a fancy office like Mr. Brady.

JOHNNY:
WHO?

Grace points to The Brady Bunch reruns playing on Nickelodeon.

GRACE (matter of fact):
Mr. Brady. Marcia's dad.

BELLA:
I talk with Senhor Silva at the factory. He say you got a job there anytime's.

JOHNNY:
Ma, I'm not gonna go work shoveling shit for a living.

(winking at Grace)
I'm gonna go work in a fancy office like Marcia's dad.

62 *INT. SPRING HILL CASKET MANUFACTURERS - DAY*

Burger King Whoppers, fries and shakes line the top of a casket. Tommy's chowing down. Smoking a joint. Alternating between bites and drags.

TOMMY CALLAHAN (talking to his Whopper):
Bacon Cheese Double Whopper. I've been dreaming of you for months.

Tommy passes Johnny the joint, Johnny shakes his head, No.

> TOMMY CALLAHAN (mouth full, to Johnny):
> *So, you in or what?*
>
> JOHNNY:
> *God, Tommy. You've been out of jail a week and you're already thinking of ways to get yourself back in!*
>
> TOMMY CALLAHAN:
> *Oh yeah, Mr. War Hero. What the frig' else am I suppose to do?*
>
> JOHNNY:
> *I don't know, Tommy. How about just playing it straight.*
>
> TOMMY CALLAHAN:
> *Doing what? Selling brooms?*

(pushes back in his chair)

> *We're never, ever gonna make any money playing it straight, man. Come on. They brainwash ya' in the Army or what? You know the system's rigged. Guys like us, we ain't ever gonna catch a break.*

63 SEQUENCE OF SHOTS:

Tommy, Fat Manny, Little Louie stealing cases of liquor out the back of Kappy's; tossing baked hams into the back of a hearse; Tommy modeling leather jackets as Louie pushes a rack full of jackets into a Spring Hill Caskets truck; Fat Manny stocking a casket full of Dora the Explorer dolls.

64 INT. AGWAY FERTILIZER FACTORY - DAY

Brown soot cakes the walls.

Sweaty men, wearing dust masks and ear plugs, fill bags with fertilizer on a fast moving conveyor belt.

65 INT. MANAGER'S OFFICE, AGWAY FERTILIZER

Johnny's sitting in front of a cheap metal desk in a tiny office. MR. SILVA - short, bald, middle-aged Portuguese man, sits behind the desk.

> MR. SILVA (Portuguese accent):
> *Your papa was a good man. You know, back in the old country, we was best friends. But he...he was the handsome one.*

... Revealing a mouthful of crowded, cigarette-stained teeth.

> MR. SILVA (tapping his head):
> *And smart, too.*

Johnny nods politely.

> MR. SILVA:
> *I gotta be straight Johnny. Times is tough. I got a hard time just keepin' the guys I got busy. But I promised your Ma.*

(passing him a dust mask)

> *I got an opening as a loadah on the skeleton crew.*

66 INT. CAREER BUILDERS EMPLOYMENT CENTER - CONTINUOUS

Chubby, middle-aged woman sporting a SuperCuts hair-do, sits behind a cluttered desk. Johnny - handsome, in a shirt and tie, sits across from her.

MRS. ABERNATHY (warm, kind):
Thank you for your service Corporal Vieira.

JOHNNY (politely):
Thank you, ma'am.

She glances at his all too short application. Looks up.

MRS. ABERNATHY:
I have to be honest with you sweetheart ... getting a decent paying job with just a GED is gonna be an uphill battle.

Turning over his application to reveal a totally blank side.

MRS. ABERNATHY:
Any chance you could go back to school? Maybe take some night classes?

67 EXT. LOADING DOCK AGWAY FERTILIZER COMPANY - NIGHT

Johnny, sweating, tosses heavy bags of fertilizer into the back of the open truck.

Radio BLARING, Tommy Callahan drives by HONKING. Laughing. Waving from a new souped-up Mustang, wearing a new leather jacket. A sexy girl, wearing a bright red leather jacket rides next to him.

Johnny SHOOTS Tommy the bird.

CUT TO:

68 INT. TOY STORE - MORNING

Fat Manny's talking non-stop. Johnny scans the dolls on the shelf.

FAT MANNY:
*He's got his head so far up her ass he don't see straight.
He wants to go and marry "Blow Job fuckin' Tracy."
I told him, Louie, Little Louie. Listen to Fat Manny
... you just can't go around marryin' them party girls.
Screw 'em yeah, but for Christ's sake, don't go and
marry them broads.*

JOHNNY (laughing):
I don't know who's more nuts, you or Little Louie.

Johnny stops, grabs a Dora the Explorer doll. Heads to the check out.

FAT MANNY:
Where ya' goin' with that?

JOHNNY:
To the cash register.

FAT MANNY:
Why?

JOHNNY (matter of fact):
To pay for it.

FAT MANNY (grabbing for the doll):
Give me that.

Johnny pulls it away from him.

FAT MANNY:
*Are you nuts? Why are you gonna pay for that. I can get
you a dozen of them stupid dolls for nothin.'*

JOHNNY:
*It's for my little sister. I ain't gonna give Grace a stolen
doll.*

69 INT. SPRING HILL CASKET MANUFACTURERS - AFTERNOON

Caskets in every shape, size and price circle Tommy holding court - sitting inside an open casket smoking a joint.

Fat Manny tosses ziplock bags of marijuana into a casket. Arms folded, Johnny leans up against the wall.

> TOMMY CALLAHAN:
> *Come on Johnny. Just say the word. I can get you in with O'Leary,*

(snapping his fingers)

> *like that!*

> JOHNNY:
> *Listen Tommy. I ain't selling drugs to little kids.*

> TOMMY CALLAHAN:
> *Who says you gotta sell drugs? There's plenty of other shit to sell. Come on Johnny, it's a ton of dough. More than you ever dreamed of.*

(taking a drag)

> *Anyway, all we're doin' is moving stuff around. You know, taking from the rich and giving to the poor. Like Robin Hood shit.*

> LITTLE LOUIE (rushing in):
> *Hey Johnny, you better get out here. Fast.*

70 EXT. SPRING HILL CASKET MANUFACTURERS

Splattered with blood, Bella and Grace rush across the street.

Blood-red paint covers their clothes, hair, faces.

Grace is crying, Bella's holding back tears as she drags Grace by the hand.

> JOHNNY:
> *What the ...?*

(running across street)

> *Ma. What happened to you?*
>
> GRACE (sobbing):
> *Them. Those bad boys. They sprayed us with paint.*

Grace wipes her runny nose with her little hand, leaving blood-red paint smeared across her tiny face.

> GRACE:
> *They just laughed and called us bad names.*

Bella breaks down, falling against Johnny, covering him in red paint.

He pulls his mom in closer. STARES out stone-faced.

71 EXT. ROOSEVELT TOWERS - LATER THAT NIGHT

A radio is BLARING.

The dilapidated, concrete Projects TOWERS in the background. Along the wall are a dozen or so tough guys and a couple of skanky girls drinking beer, smoking cigarettes, playing "Crank That" loud from a car stereo.

Across the street, Little Louie dawdles by ... alone.

> PROJECT KID:
> *Hey! You shorty. What the fuck you doin' walking on my street?*
>
> LITTLE LOUIE (stopping):
> *... You talking to me, you low life Project Faggot?*

PROJECT KID:
Yeah, you - Ass wipe. Stop stinking up my street with your Port-a-Gee B.O.

BOOM! They whip beer bottles at Louie. CHARGE at him.

Little Louie runs towards a parked van. Project Boys in hot pursuit.

Catching up, they charge Louis at the van - doors SWING open.

RUSHING OUT Johnny, Fat Manny, Tommy Callahan and some BIG tough, tattooed dudes carrying bats and chains.

Project kids SCRAMMING every which way. TOO LATE.

72 INT. VIEIRA FAMILY APARTMENT - LATER THAT NIGHT

SILENT. DARK ... except for the bathroom light shining.

Johnny's studying his blood-splattered image in the mirror: hair is messed, shirt's torn and he has blood on his hands.

GRACE:
Did those bad boys hurt you too?

CLOSE VIEW: Grace, dressed in her Barbie pajamas, standing in the doorway holding her Dora the Explorer doll.

JOHNNY:
Nope baby girl ... Not this time.

73 SEQUENCE OF SHOTS:

JOHNNY'S NOW in the thick of it with Tommy Callahan, Fat Manny and Little Louie: Spring Hill Casket Factory - packing rows of coffins full of stolen goods ... Jack Daniels to chocolates to Kitty Litter.

74 EXT. VIEIRA FIRST FLOOR PORCH - DAY

Grace and her ten-year-old friend, JOEY MEDEIROS, sit on the porch floor playing "Go Fish."

Johnny's across from them meticulously washing his car. Tommy sits on the stoop smoking and "supervising."

> TOMMY CALLAHAN (to Johnny):
> *You missed a spot.*
>
> JOHNNY (tossing a sponge at Tommy):
> *Anytime you wanna help.*

Using his mop of curly black hair to camouflage his eyes, Joey sneaks peeks at Grace's cards as he deals out the deck.

> GRACE (catching him):
> *Stop it Joey.*
>
> JOEY (continues dealing cards):
> *What? I ain't doing nothin.'*
>
> GRACE (standing up, calling over to her brother):
> *Johnny, Joey's cheating. Make him stop.*
>
> JOHNNY:
> *Joey, cut it out. You don't ever cheat your friends.*
>
> TOMMY CALLAHAN:
> *That's right. You leave that shit to screw them rich assholes.*
>
> JOHNNY:
> *Tommy. Language, come on.*

Like jail house bars, Tommy peers through the porch slats. MOTIONS Joey over to him. Gets EYEBALL to EYEBALL.

TOMMY CALLAHAN:
Listen. Rule number one, little man. If you're gonna cheat, DON'T get caught.

75 INT. VIEIRA LIVING ROOM - LATER

Grace watches TV, singing and dancing with her Dora doll.

GRACE (singing Cinderella song):
In my own little corner, in my own little chair, I can be whoever I want to be...

Door bell RINGS. Grace, holding her doll, opens the door.

POLICEMAN:
'Your mother home?

Grace nods "yes" and just stands at the door looking up at him.

POLICEMAN:
Can you get her for me?

GRACE (yelling from the door):
Momma, the police is here.

Bella appears from the kitchen, wearing an apron, drying her hands on a dish towel.

A tall, blonde, heavy-set policeman stands in the doorway, towering over her little girl.

BELLA (in Portuguese to Grace):
What does he want?

GRACE (to policeman):
What do you want?

70

> BILLY MAGUIRE (entering the apartment):
> *I'm Officer Billy Maguire. I'm investigating a report of stolen merchandise which we have cause to believe have been delivered to this house.*
>
> BELLA:
> *No. We no steal. We no crooks.*

Without asking permission, he boldly walks around the humble apartment, opening drawers and closet doors.

Grace follows, EYEING HIS EVERY MOVE, as he snoops from room to room.

Maguire points to her doll.

> BILLY MAGUIRE:
> *That new?*
>
> GRACE (holding the doll tighter):
> *Yeah. My big brother gave it to me.*
>
> BILLY MAGUIRE:
> *He give you anything else?*

Grace shields the doll behind her back.

76 EXT. CAMBRIDGE STREET

Bella - dressed in her widow's black, gripping Grace by the hand, races up the street. Grace struggles to keep up.

> GRACE:
> *WHERE are we going?*
>
> BELLA:
> *CHURCH. We go pray for Johnny.*

GRACE:
Why? What does he need?

BELLA:
He need to be a good boy. A good man. Like your Papa.

77 INT. ST. ANTHONY'S PORTUGUESE CHURCH

Except for a handful of old women dressed in their widow's black ... the church is empty.

Bella drags Grace over to the marble statue of the Virgin Mary.

From around her neck, Bella pulls at her Saint Michael medallion - kisses it, lights a candle, double blesses herself, and kneels.

Holding her miniature rosary beads, Grace imitates Bella.

BELLA (looking from the Virgin Mary to Grace):
You promise Nossa Senhora de Fatima. And swear on your papa's soul ... you always be a good girl for God.

GRACE (V.O.):
Oh yeah, that's another right of passage ... promising God, Baby Jesus, the Saint of the Day and swearing on all your dead ancestors' souls that you'll never make your momma cry. It's our version of a Portuguese pinky swear.

78 INT. VIEIRA APARTMENT KITCHEN - 3:00 AM

The sliver of light from the open refrigerator illuminates the pitch black room. Johnny reaches for a carton of milk.

A cat MEOWS.

JOHNNY:
Hey buddy.

BELLA:
Senhor Silva calls. He say you no go to work? No even calls.

JOHNNY:
Jeez Ma, you scared me.

BELLA:
Where you go if you no go to work?

JOHNNY:
No where's, I'm just hanging out.

BELLA:
What is hang out?

JOHNNY:
Ma, gimme' a break. I just got back. I need some time.

BELLA:
Time? Time for what?

He pours the milk into the cat's bowl, kisses his mother on the forehead.

JOHNNY (walking away):
Ma, I'm tired. I'm going to bed.

BELLA:
John Manuel Vieira. No forget. God sees everything.

CUT TO:

79 INT. THE SPRING HILL CASKET MANUFACTURERS - CHRISTMAS WEEK

The factory is strewn with tacky Christmas decorations. Caskets filled with everything from booze to toys - a makeshift COSTCO.

Johnny, Tommy Callahan, Fat Manny and Little Louie are all selling stolen merchandise.

Lots of CASH passing hands.

Tommy has his arm around a cute blonde girl.

> TOMMY CALLAHAN (pointing around the room):
> *Anything you want baby, I'm the man, just ask me. I taught these guys everything they know... I raised them from puppies.*

Johnny is walking up and down the casket aisles, organizing anything that's out of place.

CLOSE ON: a gold necklace chain attached to a large Holy Spirit medallion. Admiring it, Johnny turns it over and reads a Portuguese inscription.

> JOHNNY (to Fat Manny):
> *What's this?*

> FAT MANNY (shrugging):
> *I don't know. Some Saint.*

> JOHNNY:
> *I know that ... Where'd you get it?*

> FAT MANNY (nodding over):
> *Ask Little Louie. It's his stuff.*

Little Louie heads over with a wad of cash in hand.

> JOHNNY (holding up the necklace):
> *Where'd you get this?*

> LITTLE LOUIE:
> *I took it off old man Cabral.*

JOHNNY:
Did you take anything else?

LITTLE LOUIE:
Nah, everything else was crap.

Johnny moves in close to Little Louie and Fat Manny.

JOHNNY (quietly, aggressively):
You NEVER, EVER steal from your own people.

Johnny puts the chain in Louie's hand.

JOHNNY:
Put it back.

Tommy taps Johnny on the shoulder. Whispers in his ear.

80 EXT. CAMBRIDGE STREET

A shiny, black Buick with tinted windows is parked on the corner.

Inside, chain smoking cigarettes, is JIMMY O'LEARY - slim, blonde, middle-aged man with squinty dark eyes. Johnny and Tommy get in the back.

81 INT. BLACK BUICK

O'Leary takes a long puff on his cigarette, rolls down the window, tosses it out.

JIMMY O'LEARY (Boston accent, to Tommy):
I need to talk with Johnny. ALONE.

TOMMY CALLAHAN:
But, I ...

O'Leary pushes open the door. Tommy reluctantly leaves.

JIMMY O'LEARY:
Heard what you did to those Project assholes. You did good. Protecting your family always comes first. I like that in you Johnny Boy. You've been doing a good job for us ...

(tapping his temple)

You, you got brains.

Johnny listens intently.

JIMMY O'LEARY:
You know, Johnny. Really smart people, they don't know a lot. They don't ask a lot of questions ... They just keep their mouths shut and do their job.

JOHNNY:
Well then Mr. O'Leary, I guess I'm a genius.

JIMMY O'LEARY:
Good. That's the way I like it.

(pause)

But Tommy ... I'm ain't so sure about him.

JOHNNY:
But we're...

JIMMY O'LEARY (puts his left hand up):
Friends. I know. And I know he's the one that brought you in. You're pals. But he's becoming a risk ..

Druggies with big mouths ain't what I need.

(pushes a finger into Johnny's chest)

He needs to know, you don't shit where you eat.

JOHNNY:
I get it. I'll keep an eye on him.

O'Leary pulls out and lights another cigarette.

Long awkward silence.

O'Leary reaches underneath the car seat, slowly pulls out a fat envelope.

JIMMY O'LEARY (presses the envelope into Johnny):
THIS is the only friend you'll ever need.

82 INT. VIEIRA LIVING ROOM - CHRISTMAS MORNING

A 'Charlie Brown' Christmas tree decorated with silver garland and tacky Christmas decorations sits in the corner. The tree is dwarfed by the huge sea of gifts.

GRACE:
WOW! Look at what Santa brought.

Fatima walks in holding a newborn baby, with her toddler tugging at her nightgown.

FATIMA:
Oh My God!

Grace and Fatima start rummaging through the gifts - wildly tearing off wrapping paper. Bella stands at the door, arms folded across her chest.

BELLA:
Where all this stuff come from?

GRACE:
It's from Santa, Momma... I just love Santa.

Johnny appears from behind and kisses Bella's cheek.

> JOHNNY:
> *HO! HO! HO! Merry Christmas. So, Ma, what do you think?*
>
> BELLA (indignant, hurt):
> *What I think? I think I no understand where somebody who no works, gots money to buy all this things.*
>
> JOHNNY (proudly):
> *I have my connections.*

Disappointed, she stomps down the hall to her bedroom.

> JOHNNY (following his mother):
> *Ma, Ma. I did this for you. I wanna' make you happy. It's a real American Christmas, just like you always dreamed of.*
>
> BELLA (tearing up):
> *I no ever dreams of this. We no come to America to steal. To be crooks. We leave our home. Our country because of men who do these bad things.*

(continues adamantly in Portuguese)

> *I want all these evil things out of my house. NOW! Not one thing stays here. You have already disgraced yourself, but you will not dishonor me or the memory of your father like this.*

She SLAMS the door in his face.

83 INT. JOHNNY'S CAR - LATE NIGHT

The back seat is filled with ALL the Christmas presents. Johnny's driving. Tommy's smoking a joint.

JOHNNY:
I thought she'd be happy.

TOMMY CALLAHAN (taking a drag):
Yeah, she spoiled your whole friggin' Christmas.

SIRENS BLARING.

Johnny's rearview mirror: Police car's red lights flashing, signaling for him to pull over. Out walks a tall, heavy-set young cop.

JOHNNY:
Oh, shit. Roll down the windows. Quick.

The officer points the flashlight directly into Johnny and Tommy's eyes. Johnny covers his eyes.

JOHNNY:
Hey, cut the shit Maguire.

Officer Billy Maguire points the light into the back seat.

BILLY MAGUIRE:
That's Officer Maguire to you. You got a receipt for these, J-J-J- Johnny?

JOHNNY:
Grow up Billy.

Billy points the flashlight at Tommy.

BILLY MAGUIRE:
Where's the dope?

TOMMY CALLAHAN (sarcastically):
I'm looking right at him.

BILLY MAGUIRE (pulling out his gun):
O.K. Get out of the car. NOW!

JOHNNY:
AH! Come on Maguire. It's Christmas for Christ sake.

Johnny slowly leans across towards the glove compartment, pulls out a big bag of weed and a wad of cash. Hands it to Maguire.

Maguire pockets the dope and the money.

BILLY MAGUIRE (looking at Tommy):
Next time Tommy, keep your big, fat mouth shut.

Tommy leans over and BLOWS a cloud of smoke from his joint RIGHT into Maguire's face.

BILLY MAGUIRE (waving his gun):
That's it! Both of you. Out of the car. In the spirit of Christmas, I'm just busting you for possession of stolen goods.

(looking at Tommy)

Now who's the dope, Callahan?

84 INT. CAMBRIDGE POLICE STATION, FRONT DESK - NEXT MORNING

Grace and Bella stand in front of a high, glassed-in police station counter.

It TOWERS over Grace. A big burly, old-timer cop slides open the glass partition.

POLICEMAN (to Bella):
Yeah, what can I do for ya'?

The cop HEARS a little voice coming from below the counter.

GRACE:
Hello. Excuse me.

He rises, peers down: Grace wearing a little red Santa hat. She WAVES UP at him. Smiles.

> GRACE:
> *Excuse me Mr. Policeman. We're here to bring my big brother home.*

Shaking his head, the burly cop MORPHS into a teddy bear.

> POLICEMAN:
> *Okay doll face. Who's your brother?*
>
> GRACE:
> *Johnny.*
>
> POLICEMAN:
> *Johnny what?*
>
> GRACE (confused):
> *What?*
>
> POLICEMAN:
> *Your brother. What's his last name?*
>
> GRACE:
> *Oh. Vieira. Johnny Vieira.*
>
> POLICEMAN (looking down at the log):
> *He's been arrested for possession of stolen goods. His bail's set at $1,500.*

Bella reaches into a brown paper bag, pulling out money.

> BELLA:
> *We got monies.*
>
> POLICEMAN (holding his hand up):
> *NO. NO. Not here.*

(speed talking)

> *Go down the hall, first right, take a left and it's the third door on your right marked "Bail Bondsman." They'll take care of you down there.*

BELLA (tearing up, confused):
I no understand.

GRACE (taking her mother by the hand):
It's okay momma. I can find it. Come with me.

85 EXT. POLICE STATION

Johnny exits the police station holding Grace's hand. Bella - red-faced, fuming - is quick at their heels.

BELLA (Portuguese):
How? How could you shame your family like this? I had to go and ask Senhor Silva for money to get you out of jail.

(shouts)

> *FOR STEALING!*

Johnny speeds up, keeping his distance. Grace hurries to stay up with him.

GRACE (looking up):
Johnny, Momma says only bad boys go to jail.

Johnny looks away.

Bella catches up to them.

BELLA:
Thanks God your papa's not here to see the kind of man you become.

Johnny STOPS. CRUSHED.

> JOHNNY (slowly, deliberately):
> *I've got nothing else, Ma.*

(wiping his eyes)

> *Can't you see. There's nothin' else out here for guys like me.*

Tearing up, Bella clutches the brown paper bag to her chest - feeling the loss of Jose and the weight of how much coming to America has cost her family.

> GRACE (V.O.):
> *That was the last time my brother brought his work home and the last time our family ever talked about it.*

86 INT. SPRING HILL CASKET MANUFACTURERS - DAY

A stone-faced O'Leary sits behind his large, oak desk, chain-smoking.

Billy Maguire stands in front - nervously shuffling his feet. Johnny and Tommy sit across from them on the couch.

> JIMMY O'LEARY (livid, to Maguire):
> *What the hell's wrong with you, Maguire?*

(pointing towards the couch)

> *You know those guys work for me. What the fuck were you thinking?*
>
> BILLY MAGUIRE (mumbling):
> *I, I just thought ...*
>
> JIMMY O'LEARY (interrupting):
> *Shut up! I don't give a shit what you think.*

(pointing his finger at Maguire)

> *You want this arrangement of ours to continue, then you better put your fucking differences aside.*

BILLY MAGUIRE:
I'm sorry Mr. O'Leary. It won't happen again.

TOMMY CALLAHAN (taunting):
Yeah, what were you thinking Maguire?

O'Leary hurls an ash tray at Tommy, barely missing his head.

JIMMY O'LEARY:
You shut your fuckin' pie hole before I shut it for you! Your old man and me may go way back ...

(turns back to Maguire)

> *... yours too. But they never did stupid shit like this. And, God rest their souls, if they was here right now, they'd be kicking the crap out of you.*

(turns again and waves a dismissing hand)

> *ALL of you'se - get the fuck out of my sight.*

ACT 3

BACK TO PRESENT DAY

87 CHEERING CROWD, CAMBRIDGE, MA

Johnny and 20-year-old Grace (whom we met in the opening scene) sit CHEERING at a Boston Celtics game, eating hot dogs and sporting a green "Celtics #1" foam finger.

> GRACE (V.O.):
> *I know my brother did some bad things. But sometimes, good people do stupid things.*

(a beat)

> *You see – to me, he was just my big brother. He had a way of making my life seem normal. You know. More American.*

CUT TO:

88 INT. CABRAL'S NEW ATOMIC FISH MARKET - DAY

Cabral's tiny market has EXPANDED - glassed-in counters brimming with fresh, whole fish on ice, octopus, crabs, sardines. Piles of dried cod line a whole counter.

The store is packed with working-class Portuguese ladies buying fish - neatly dressed in colorful house dresses, maids uniforms, and of course, widow's black.

It's LOUD. Everyone's SPEAKING AND ORDERING in Portuguese.

> MULTIPLE CUSTOMERS (Portuguese ordering):
> *Dam dues libras de abroita.*
>
> *Nao, nao. Eu quero o polv fresco.*
>
> *Mas caranguejos.*

The store door bell JANGLES.

The ladies turn as ALEX MCPHEARSON enters the doorway - tall, blonde and a bit too good looking.

(Late 20's) - Wearing a Harvard Crimson tie, Brooks Brothers navy blue blazer, Alex nods politely to the GAPING women.

Not only is he the ONLY male customer, but with his light blonde features - he stands totally out of place among the dark-haired, working class women.

Alex walks towards the counter as the women watch him order - IN ENGLISH.

> ALEX MCPHEARSON (too polite to be from Boston):
> *May I please have half a pound of salmon.*
>
> COUNTER CLERK (pointing to the wrong fish):
> *Este aqui.*
>
> ALEX MCPHEARSON:
> *No, no. The one next to it, please.*

The Clerk grabs a whole salmon.

ALEX MCPHEARSON:
Yes, yes that's it.

The clerk weighs the fish on the scale, turns to wrap it up. Whole.

ALEX MCPHEARSON (making a cutting motion):
No, excuse me. Sir. I need it CUT. Filleted. Just one little piece.

The clerk continues wrapping up the fish.

ALEX MCPHEARSON (speaking a bit louder):
FILET! Filet. CUT. IN PIECES.

Everyone in the store is buying their fish whole. The clerk doesn't understand.

Frustrated. Alex turns around, raising his hands in the air.

ALEX MCPHEARSON:
Does anyone in here speak English?

Fellow shopper Grace (20), taps him on the shoulder.

GRACE (smiling, amused):
Maybe I can help.

Turning around, Alex finds a grinning Grace ... wearing a 'Made in Portugal, Assembled in the USA' t-shirt and shorts.

She knocks him off track for a second with her smiling eyes and sweet face.

ALEX MCPHEARSON:
OH... Thank goodness, you speak English.

GRACE (to the Clerk, in Portuguese):
Ele quer ou peixe cortado, uma libra. Por favor, Senhor Amaral.

> COUNTER CLERK (nodding):
> *Ahhh sim. Okay, Grace. Está bom.*
>
> GRACE (to Alex):
> *You're all set.*
>
> ALEX MCPHEARSON:
> *How? Thank you. Thank you so much.*
>
> GRACE:
> *Sure. No problem.*

She smiles. Leaves. Alex stands there. Unknowingly smiling, looking at her as she walks down the street.

CUT TO:

89 *INT. FATIMA AND EDDIE'S KITCHEN*

Her back to the door, Fatima washes dishes at the sink. The door OPENS. SLAMS shut. She JUMPS.

Eddie's trudging in, tearing open his bus driver uniform shirt, buttons popping off everywhere.

He rips it off and tosses the shirt across the kitchen floor.

> FATIMA:
> *What's wrong?*
>
> EDDIE
> *20 years. Not one fucking sick day off.*

STUNNED. He throws himself into a chair.

> EDDIE:
> *Boom. Just like that, we're garbage on the street.*

Fatima, wiping her wet hands on her apron.

FATIMA:
What happened, Eddie?

EDDIE:
Me, Mario and ten other guys. We just got laid off. No notice. No nothin.'

(uncharacteristically tearing up)

And, and ... just like that, they took away my keys.

FATIMA (walking closer):
It's gonna be okay. You'll find another job.

(Eddie rubbed his eyes, trying to conceal his overwhelming loss)

EDDIE:
No. You don't get it. That was MY BUS.

(a beat)

That job. It was the only thing I've ever been good at.

Eddie falls weeping against Fatima's damp apron.

90 EXT. SPRING HILL CASKETS - CONTINUOUS

As Johnny and Fat Manny turn the corner, a HUMAN FIREBALL BOLTS out the side door - running down the alley. SCREAMING.

JOHNNY:
What the...

Fat Manny takes off down the alley after the streak of flames. Johnny YANKS open the door.

91 INT. SPRING HILL CASKETS

A casket packed with plastic bags of cocaine is on fire. Little Louie's whacking the fire with his jacket.

Tommy's FREEBASING cocaine from the top of a nearby casket.

> TOMMY CALLAHAN (stoned):
> *Yeah. When I die, I'm gonna be buried face down so you can all KISS MY WHITE IRISH ASS!*

> JOHNNY (loudly):
> *What the fuck are you guys doing?*

Johnny grabs the fire extinguisher from the corner - puts out the fire.

> JOHNNY:
> *How STUPID can you guys be?*

> TOMMY CALLAHAN:
> *Hey? WHO farted and made you king?*

> JOHNNY (to Little Louie):
> *Hurry up. Clean up this shit before ...*

O'Leary walks in.

92 *EXT. VIEIRA FIRST FLOOR PORCH - NEXT MORNING*

Bella and Senhora CABRAL sit on the porch knitting and chattering away in Portuguese.

His black curly hair framing his big brown eyes, JOEY MEDEIROS (now 20) - Grace's boyfriend - LEAPS onto the porch with a mischievous smile. STARTLING them.

> BELLA:
> *Aí Corisco Diabo!*

She reaches over, playfully taps him with her knitting needles on his head.

BELLA:
Joey. Juízo na cabeça. You too big a boy to play like this.

JOEY (Blue Collar accent):
I know you still love me best Senhora Vieira.

He kisses Bella on the cheek.

Where's Grace? Where's my girl?

93 INT. BELLA'S SEWING ROOM

The same flowered curtain serves as the door to Bella's sewing room. In the corner, sits the old Singer sewing machine across from the daybed. Grace's Dora the Explorer doll rests on a pillow.

Grace is halfway under the daybed, her dark tanned legs peeking out. Joey reaches down and tickles her bare feet.

Grace looks up from underneath.

GRACE:
Hey Joey. You're early.

JOEY:
I know. I gotta make a stop before I drop you off.

Grace continues searching under the bed.

JOEY:
What are you lookin' for?

GRACE:
My ring. I can't find it anywhere.

(pointing to the sewing machine)

I put it right on top of there last night.

JOEY:
Don't worry about it.

GRACE:
Joey. That's my promise ring. You paid a lot of money for it.

He reaches down for her hand, helping her up.

GRACE:
I really love that ring...

(taking one last look around)

Maybe I should pray to that Saint who finds stuff?

JOEY:
Forget about it. I'll just buy you another one.

GRACE:
With what?

(pinching his cheeks)

Your good looks?

He takes her hand from his cheek, kisses it. Then pulls out a big wad of cash from his pants pocket.

JOEY:
With this. I got lucky at the dog track last night.

GRACE:
Joey, be good. You blew a ton of money there last time.

JOEY (smiling, charming):
Good ... I've always been.

94 INT. CHARLESBANK DRY CLEANERS - CONTINUOUS

Turtle's at the counter, his shirt hanging out of his pants - a six pack of Sagres beer in one hand and a crumpled paper bag in the other.

Wearing a bright pink sundress, Grace enters carrying a pile of clothing - all neatly pressed, folded over hangers.

> GRACE:
> *Hey, Turtle. I brought back all my mom's alterations.*
>
> TURTLE (admiring the pile):
> *That ma of yours - she ain't only good, she's fast.*

Grace places the clothing on a nearby rack, walks towards Turtle and glances at the crumpled paper bag he's holding.

> GRACE:
> *Turtle, you're the only person I know who carries his cash around in a brown paper bag.*
>
> TURTLE:
> *Hey, whose gonna hold up a fat old guy with a dirty paper bag?*
>
> GRACE:
> *Anything I need to know today?*
>
> TURTLE:
> *Nope, "NADA" I'm goin' to Newton. Somebody's stealing again. Stupids!! I give 'em jobs and they clean my watch.*
>
> GRACE (laughing):
> *Clock, Turtle. It's clean my clock.*
>
> TURTLE:
> *What? Clock, watch? Don't matter to me. Stealing's stealin.'*

Turtle heads out the back. Grace kneels down behind the counter yanking at a blue nylon laundry bag.

Alex McPhearson, dapper in a Ralph Lauren polo and immaculately pressed khakis, enters carrying a bundle of shirts.

Grace pops up from behind the counter - a vision in pink. Alex immediately recognizes her.

> ALEX MCPHEARSON (friendly):
> *Hi there.*

Grace smiles.

> GRACE (politely):
> *Hi.*
>
> ALEX MCPHEARSON:
> *Aren't you the girl from the fish market?*
>
> GRACE (looks at him quizzically):
> *Excuse me?*
>
> ALEX MCPHEARSON:
> *You, you helped me the other day. At the fish market. In Inman Square. Remember?*
>
> GRACE:
> *Oh yeah. The filet guy.*

She starts counting out his shirts.

> ALEX MCPHEARSON:
> *So how did you learn Portuguese?*
>
> GRACE:
> *I'm Portuguese. I came here as a baby.*

(pause)

> *What's your name?*

He looks pleased that she has asked.

> ALEX MCPHEARSON (excited):
> *Alex.*

Sees her head is down, waiting to write his name on the slip.

> ALEX MCPHEARSON (embarrassed):
> *Oh, Alex, Alex McPhearson.*

> GRACE:
> *How do you like them?*

> ALEX MCPHEARSON:
> *Excuse me?*

> GRACE:
> *Your shirts?*

> ALEX MCPHEARSON:
> *Oh, um, boxed, no starch please.*

Grace counts out his shirts.

> GRACE:
> *Okay. Six shirts, boxed, no starch. How's Wednesday?*

> ALEX MCPHEARSON:
> *Fine, sure ... that works.*

95 *EXT. CHARLESBANK DRY CLEANERS*

Outside the dry cleaners entrance, Alex slowly looks back through the glass door - lingering a little too long on Grace as she stuffs his shirts into the blue nylon bag.

96 INT. BELLA'S SEWING ROOM - NIGHT, LATER

The "whirring" of the old-fashioned Singer fills the small room as Bella sits sewing.

Grace peeks in through the curtain.

> GRACE:
> *Bye Ma. I'm off with Joey.*

Bella turns around smiling, her face instantly dissolves into disapproval.

Grace is dressed in a short black skirt, skimpy top and black ankle-high boots. She looks HOT!

> BELLA (broken English):
> *NO, NO, NO. You no go out this way.*
>
> GRACE:
> *What "way?"*

Grace admires herself in the full length mirror.

> *Ma, I look great. This is what everybody's wearing.*
>
> BELLA:
> *I no care. You no look like a lady.*
>
> GRACE (pleading):
> *Ma, come on. I'm already late.*
>
> BELLA:
> *GRACE Isabel Vieira. You listen to your mama. Is better to be a whore and dress like a lady, then to be a lady and dress like a whore.*

(shaking her head)

God NO likes.

GRACE:
Oh my God. Where do you come up with this stuff?

(walking away)

Maybe I should just wear a burka. That should make God happy.

97 INT. SPRING HILL CASKET MANUFACTURERS - NIGHT

A "Towns & Gowns" party is in HOT progress: Beautiful women, macho townies, Harvard preppies drinking, doing coke, smoking pot. All mingling among the converted caskets - transformed into bar tops and beds.

Tommy, Fat Manny and two college-age, preppy girls sit side- by-side in coffins.

Fat Manny is bulging out of his coffin.

The girls, sharing a coffin, are stoned. Snorting lines of cocaine from the top of a thick college text book.

Tommy slowly looks over from one girl to another.

TOMMY CALLAHAN (to Fat Manny):
DRUGS ... they have a way of making us all EQUALS.

98 INT. DRY CLEANERS - NEXT DAY

Her olive skin peaking through the holes of her white, eyelet blouse, Grace's hunched over the counter reading a large textbook - a pink sharpie highlighter in hand.

Alex walks in, happy to see her again.

ALEX MCPHEARSON:
Hey. What are you reading?

GRACE (matter-of-fact):
The History of Statistical Economics.

ALEX MCPHEARSON (surprised):
For fun?

GRACE:
No, for school.

ALEX MCPHEARSON:
So you work here AND go to school?

GRACE:
Yep. That's how the other half rolls.

ALEX MCPHEARSON:
No kidding? I didn't realize they were teaching senior level economics at community college? Are you at Bunker Hill?

Grace RAISES her eyebrows, about to correct him.

GRACE:
I go to...

Instead, she plays along - he's just another Cambridge Elitist Snob.

Yeah. Bunker Hill. You'd be surprised to see what they're teaching at community college these days.

A bit taken with her, he starts counting out his shirts.

ALEX MCPHEARSON (flirting a little):
So, when do you have time for fun?

GRACE (writing out his ticket):
I don't.

ALEX MCPHEARSON:
What are you studying?

GRACE:
Poli-Sci and History.

ALEX MCPHEARSON (toying with her):
Oh no. Don't tell me you want to be a lawyer.

Grace smiles, playing along, writing out his ticket.

GRACE:
What's wrong with lawyers?

Alex holds up his hands, liking her more as their conversation continues.

ALEX MCPHEARSON:
Nothing. Some of my best friends are lawyers...
Well, not really.

Laughing, she hands him his ticket.

Alex heads towards the door. Hesitates. Turns back around.

ALEX MCPHEARSON:
Uhmm. Do you have a name?

GRACE:
Grace. Grace Vieira.

ALEX MCPHEARSON:
Well, I was wondering, Grace Vieira. Do you ever have time to eat?

GRACE:
Of course.

ALEX MCPHEARSON:
Well, how about lunch sometime? Maybe you could help change my opinion of lawyers.

Grace blushes, smiling.

99 INT. INDUSTRIAL BACK OF DRY CLEANERS - CONTINUOUS

A blur of white cotton, Grace glides past the steamy, dingy laundry room packed tight with over-flowing baskets of dirty laundry.

TURTLE (angry):
Here's 200 bucks. This is the last time, Joey. Don't ask me again.

Grace walks up behind them.

GRACE:
Hey. Is everything ok?

JOEY (not expecting her):
Uhmmm ... Yeah. It's fine.

GRACE:
Okay. I'm ready to go. Everything's locked up.

Grace starts to walk away, stops and turns around.

GRACE:
Hey Turtle. Today was a really big day. We made over two thousand dollars.

TURTLE (chuckling):
Yeah. I think them college boys is bringin' in their clean clothes just to take a look at you.

Joey reaches over and pulls up the sides of Grace's off the shoulder blouse, covering her up.

She SLAPS Joey's hands away and pulls the sides back down.

100 INT. JOEY'S CAR - CONTINUOUS

GRACE:
What were you and Turtle talking about?

JOEY:
Nothing.

GRACE:
It sounded like you were arguing.

JOEY (uncharacteristically irritated):
God, Grace! He's my uncle. Can't a guy just talk to his uncle?

Grace stares down at her ringless left hand, nervously circling her ring finger with her thumb.

101 EXT. SEEDY APARTMENT

A Rottweiler's tied up to a chain link fence - BARKING.

Joey and Grace roll up, park in front of the dumpy complex.

102 INT. JOEY'S CAR

GRACE:
Why are we stopping here?

JOEY:
Um, I need to make a quick stop. Wait here.

> GRACE (looking around):
> *Maybe, I should go in with you.*
>
> JOEY:
> *No, no. Stay in the car. You'll be fine. Just lock the doors.*

Joey exits.

She locks all the car doors.

Joey's on the front porch, ringing the doorbell.

It's opened by a short, ugly guy with long, bushy hair.

> SCUMMY GUY (menacingly):
> *You alone?*
>
> JOEY:
> *Yeah, yeah. It's just me.*

He looks over Joey's shoulder to the running car.

> SCUMMY GUY:
> *Who's that?*
>
> JOEY:
> *Just my girlfriend.*

GUY takes a LONG look at her. Grace double checks all the car door locks and turns the radio up louder, looking all around.

103 INT. JOEY'S SMALL STUDIO APARTMENT - LATER

Joey whistles as he inserts a key into the lock.

The door swings open into a dark apartment.

> JOHNNY:
> *Where you been?*

Startled, Joey drops a white, canvas carpenter's bag on the floor.

Johnny's sitting on the couch in the dark.

> JOEY:
> *Jesus Christ, you scared the shit out of me.*

Joey flicks on the light.

> JOHNNY (more aggressively):
> *I asked you a question. Where were you tonight?*
>
> JOEY:
> *I was with your sister. We went out for Chinese.*
>
> JOHNNY:
> *Where else Joey?*
>
> JOEY:
> *No place.*

Johnny LUNGES towards Joey and throws him up against the wall, HARD. Grabs him tight by his jacket collar.

> JOHNNY:
> *Listen to me you little shit. I know your every move. Gambling's bad enough. But drugs. They're way out of your bush-ass league.*
>
> JOEY:
> *But, but...*
>
> JOHNNY (grabbing him tighter):
> *Don't you fuckin' BUT me. If you ever, EVER bring my sister anywhere near drugs. I'll fuckin' kill ya.'*
>
> JOEY:
> *John, Johnny. I didn't know what else to do. I owe Fat Manny two grand.*

Johnny opens up the carpenter's bag. Spots a large brick of marijuana wrapped in plastic.

> JOHNNY:
> *How'd you get the money to buy this shit? And how the hell did you plan on selling it, you fuckin' idiot.*

> JOEY:
> *I don't know. I wasn't thinking.*

> JOHNNY:
> *You listen to me good, Joey. This time, I'll take care of Fat Manny.*

Johnny grabs the bag. Points his finger at Joey.

> JOHNNY:
> *BUT YOU, you better clean up your act. You're goin' down a bad fuckin' place. And, you AIN'T taking my sister down there with ya.'*

104 INT. SPRING HILL CASKET MANUFACTURERS - NIGHT PITCH BLACK

Florescent lights flickering.

Johnny drops the carpenter bag on the desk, falls into the chair and rubs his forehead exhausted. Looking over ...

A man's hand is hanging out of an open casket.

Johnny slowly approaches ...

Tommy Callahan lies in the casket with an open bag of cocaine spread open on his chest - white coke dust covering his nose and face.

> JOHNNY:
> *What the...*

(shaking Tommy)

> *Tommy! Tommy! Wake up Man!*

Tommy doesn't move. FRANTIC, Johnny scans the room.

SPOTS the fire extinguisher. Grabs it. Sprays and covers Tommy in foam.

Tommy's coughing and flaying his arms in the air, looking like the Michelin Man.

> TOMMY CALLAHAN:
> *What the fuck you doin' to me, man?*

Johnny grabs Tommy by the collar, SHAKES him.

> JOHNNY:
> *What the hell are you doin' to YOURSELF, Tommy?*

> TOMMY CALLAHAN:
> *Fuck you, Johnny. If it wasn't for me you'd still be shoveling shit for old man Silva.*

> JOHNNY:
> *That's right Tommy. You've made my life world-class.*

Johnny HURLS the half empty bag of coke at Tommy's head.

> JOHNNY:
> *Sorry for giving a fuck.*

> > > > > > > > *CUT TO:*

105 INT. TUFTS UNIVERSITY AUDITORIUM - DAY

At the far back of a packed college auditorium near an EXIT sign, Grace sits reading a financial aid letter.

She folds it over and tucks it under her notebook.

The name of the class is written on a large white board ...

The Hidden Injuries of Class and Religion

Grace looks up ... does a DOUBLE-TAKE.

Substituting today: Assistant Professor Alex McPhearson

> ALEX MCPHEARSON (engaging):
> *I'm filling in for Professor Williams. She had a baby boy last night. He decided it was his time to shine.*

Class snickers.

Assistant Professor Alex McPhearson, in an ADHD fashion, speaks and writes on the board simultaneously, constantly turning from board to students - think a great TED Talk.

> ALEX MCPHEARSON (lively, born presenter):
> *CLASS defines the pecking order of where you stand in society.*

(turns to class, a bit irreverent)

> *You are either a big shot at the top of the heap, like Mr. Appleton over here.*

Points to a smug looking, trust fund type sitting ram rod straight in the front row.

> ALEX MCPHEARSON:
> *Or a lowly assistant professor at the bottom of the heap like me.*

Class laughs.

ALEX MCPHEARSON:
So SOCIETY and CLASS help define your self worth. RELIGION on the other hand, tells you how you should
- BEHAVE.
- ACT.
- THINK.

Religion is designed to judge you. Keep you scared. So you stay on the right path. The path that it CHOOSES for you. Organized religion is like a spiritual dictator.

(mockingly drills a hole into his skull)

Constantly drilling into your head that MY imaginary friend is better than YOUR imaginary friend.

(turns back to draw a diagram on the board)

So here we have SOCIETY and CLASS determining your self worth and place. While RELIGION over here wants to keep you fearful.

ALEX MCPHEARSON (turns to class):
Why is that?

CLASS (collectively shouts out):
CONTROL!

ALEX MCPHEARSON:
Yes. Control. See. Your parents' money isn't going to waste after all.

Classroom groans.

EXCEPT for Grace who SHIFTS uncomfortably in her seat - HIDING the financial aid letter further under her notebook.

Professor McPhearson continues writing on the white board in BIG exaggerated letters:

Control + Domination = Subordination

Close view on Grace's notebook: She writes in big capital letters, and underlines it twice:

SUBORDINATION

The class empties out around Grace.

She picks up her books and heads up to the front of the class.

Alex has his back to her, erasing the board.

> GRACE:
> *Hi.*

Alex turns around. CONFUSED.

> ALEX MCPHEARSON:
> *Hey! Hi Grace. What are you doing here?*
>
> GRACE:
> *I go here. I'm in this class.*

(holding up her book)

> ALEX MCPHEARSON:
> *Here? You go here? You're in this class? I thought you went to Bunker Hill.*
>
> GRACE:
> *Yeah. Just the shirt girl, right? ... Community college material. I couldn't possibly be in THIS class and go HERE.*

ALEX MCPHEARSON:
No, no. That's not it at all.

GRACE:
You know - this class, you ... all kinda reminds me of this old Portuguese saying: "The rich people on the mainland, they own the boats. And us poor people in the Azores, we work their boats."

(a beat)

You probably thought I could only work the boats.

Clutching her books tight, Grace turns and hurries away.

ALEX MCPHEARSON:
No, Grace. Come on ...

106 INT. VIEIRA FAMILY KITCHEN - EARLY EVENING

Bella's, in the corner, ironing Grace's graduation gown.

Grace, Fatima, Eddie, and their kids sit around the kitchen table eating fried dough ... malasadas.

Johnny walks in, kisses Bella, heads towards Grace.

JOHNNY:
I've always wanted to hug a college graduate.

They hug, she kisses him on the cheek.

JOHNNY:
Hmmm, I feel smarter already.

EDDIE:
Yeah, she's gonna go get her Bullshit of Arts degree.

Eddie laughs hysterically. No one else laughs.

> JOHNNY:
> *Shut up, Eddie. You couldn't even cut it as a bus driver.*

Eddie's laughter turns into embarrassed silence. He clenches his jaw in pure hatred towards Johnny.

> JOHNNY (whispers to Grace):
> *Walk out with me.*

107 EXT. VIERIA FRONT PORCH

Grace and Johnny share the front stoop.

> JOHNNY:
> *What a piece of shit.*

> GRACE:
> *Such a jerk ... what does Fatima see in him?*

> JOHNNY (shooting her a "speaking of jerks" look):
> *Listen, we need to talk about Joey.*

> GRACE:
> *Why? What's there to talk about?*

> JOHNNY:
> *Grace, Joey ain't a bad kid, but he's into some guys for a lot of money.*

> GRACE:
> *Money? Money for what?*

> JOHNNY:
> *Gambling.*

> GRACE:
> *What? Wait ... he said he was just having some fun.*

JOHNNY:
Yeah, a little more fun than he can afford.

GRACE:
How bad can it be? I'll talk to him. I can make him stop.

JOHNNY:
Baby Girl, be careful.

(pause)

You've made it bigger than anybody else in this whole family. Don't go screwing it all up trying to fix Joey Medeiros.

108 *INT. FATIMA AND EDDIE'S KITCHEN – MORNING*

A six pack of beer rests next to Eddie on the kitchen table. He has a beer in one hand and staring at a piece of paper in his other hand.

FATIMA:
Eddie. Come on. It's ten o'clock in the morning.

He guzzles the rest of the beer. Slams the bottle on the table. Holds up the paper.

EDDIE:
What's this?

Fatima moves in to get a closer look.

FATIMA:
Oh? That. It's an application. Market Basket's hiring cashiers. I was thinkin,' maybe I could help bring in some money. You know, until you get another job.

Eddie crumples the application. Tosses it at her bare feet.

EDDIE:
What? Now you're gonna wear the pants in the family?

FATIMA:
No. No Eddie. It was a surprise. I just wanna help.

She bends to pick up the crumpled paper. He grabs her wrist. She pushes his hand away. He grabs her other wrist. Her tiny wrists disappear into the vise grip of his big hands.

FATIMA:
Eddie. Stop. You're hurtin' me.

She struggles as he continues holding her tighter.

EDDIE:
I can take care of my own fuckin' family.

He shoves her away. Grabs the pack of beer SMASHES it on the floor.

Beer oozes out through the broken glass, spreading all over the floor - rolling towards Fatima's bare feet.

EDDIE:
You wanna work? Here you go. Clean up on Aisle Five!

109 *INT. JOEY'S APARTMENT*

The radio's PLAYING. The shower's RUNNING. Joey's SINGING from the shower.

Walking into the apartment, Grace nearly trips over Joey's construction boots and tool belt wedged by the door. Work clothes are scattered all around.

GRACE (yells out):
Hey, Joey. It's me.

Setting her books down, she picks up his clothes, carries them over to the hamper. Checking his pockets, she pulls out keys, crumpled dollar bills and a WAD of lottery tickets.

SHOWER TURNS OFF.

Joey's standing at the bathroom door with just a towel wrapped around his muscular waist. His curly wet hair framing his cute face.

> JOEY:
> *Hey babe. When'd you get here?*
>
> GRACE (flustered):
> *Just a few minutes ago.*
>
> JOEY:
> *I'll be out in a second.*

She just stares from Joey to the lottery tickets, back to him.

110 INT. JOEY'S KITCHEN - CONTINUOUS

Waiting. Grace, raps her fingers on the cheap aluminum table.

Joey - topless, wearing jeans - leans in to give her a kiss. She pulls away.

> JOEY:
> *What's up with you?*

She holds out her hand filled with the lottery tickets.

> GRACE:
> *This is what's up with me.*
>
> JOEY:
> *Grace, baby, my number is gonna hit any day. Just think about how much money I could win? We'd be set for life.*

GRACE (angry):
Where the hell did you get 500 dollars to blow on stupid lottery tickets?

JOEY (sheepish):
Oh. I got a raise.

GRACE:
Guess you forgot to tell me ...

(pause)

Nice going, Joey.

JOEY:
Come on, they're just lottery tickets. That ain't like real gambling.

GRACE:
You're an idiot.

111 INT. CLOTHING STORE BATHING SUIT SECTION - LATER THAT DAY

Searching through racks of bathing suits, Grace is pulling out bikinis, Fatima's picking through old lady one-pieces.

FATIMA:
What are ya' talking about? Joey's a great kid. He lets you do whatever you want.

GRACE:
He LETS ME ??? Are you kidding me?

FATIMA:
Come on. You know how Portuguese guys are. What's a little gambling ... You got a good one.

GRACE:
Who says he has to be Portuguese? Why can't he be Italian, or Jewish, or even Black?

FATIMA:
Oh, yeah right - Ma would love that. Grace, you're starting to dream a little too big for yourself. Don't go forgettin' where you come from.

(pause)

Remember. We always stick with our own kind.

GRACE:
Yeah. Like Eddie.

Fatima picks up an ugly, flowered bathing suit with a skirted bottom - perfect for a nun.

Fatima's bruised wrist peeks out from under her sleeve.

GRACE (reaching for Fatima's wrist):
What happened to your wrist?

Fatima drops the bathing suit and quickly adjusts her sleeve.

FATIMA:
Nothing. I slipped on the carpet.

GRACE: (shooting her a look)
Yeah. Okay. Sure you did.

(flipping through suits)

I hate shopping for bathing suits with you. Every year, it's the same old thing.

(mimicking Eddie)

> *No, that's too revealing, too tight, too low, too high ... Why did you marry stupid Eddie anyway?*

> FATIMA (with her back to Grace):
> *I was 16, pregnant. Hardly spoke English.*

(pause)

> *It was a long time ago.*

(facing Grace)

> *You got pregnant, you got married. That's what you did back then.*

Fatima goes back to flipping through bathing suits.

> GRACE:
> *Did you love him?*

> FATIMA:
> *Yeah, I really did. Stupid me, I still do.*

Grace comes around holding a beautiful red one-piece bathing suit, totally appropriate for a mom.

> GRACE:
> *You'd look great in this.*

> FATIMA (laughing):
> *Yeah right. He'd never let me out of the house in that.*

Fatima heads into the dressing room, armed with a dozen nun worthy bathing suits. Grace plops the red bathing suit on top.

CUT TO:

112 EXT. APARTMENT ROOF TOP - JULY 4TH NIGHT

LOUD MUSIC. Dancing. Drinking. Smoking Dope.

Dozens of guys and girls are partying on top of the apartment's roof. Fat Manny and Little Louie are totally wasted.

113 INT. DARKENED BATHROOM

Johnny turns the knob on an old, scarred-up door, opening it up into a darkened bathroom.

Turns on the light. STOPS.

With his back to the door, hair matted and dirty under a black P.O.W. bandana, Tommy is sitting on top of the toilet seat. A rubber tube's wrapped around his left arm. He's holding a syringe in his right hand.

> JOHNNY:
> *What the fuck, Tommy?*

Tommy jumps and slowly cranes his head towards Johnny. His face is thin and gaunt, his eyes bloodshot. Distant.

He swivels around, looking Johnny STRAIGHT in the eye.

> TOMMY CALLAHAN (his words slow and deliberate):
> *You don't know a damn thing about it. It's the prettiest high you'll ever get. It's like seeing the fuckin' Virgin Mary.*

Tommy deliberately sticks the syringe into his veined arm as his head rolls backwards, sinking back against the toilet.

Johnny steadies himself up against the doorframe, eyes tearing up as he helplessly WATCHES his best friend disappear into his high.

114 EXT. APARTMENT ROOF TOP - NIGHT, A FEW HOURS LATER

In the background, colorful fire works BURST and CRACKLE. The blast of colors adding to the party's HIGH.

> FAT MANNY (visibly high, pointing, laughing):
> *Oh shit man! Look at Tommy. He thinks he's a friggin' rocket.*

Standing a little too close to the edge of the roof, Tommy's stretching out - reaching out for the fireworks.

Arms spread wide - Tommy starts flying around the roof.

EVERYONE'S POINTING OVER AT TOMMY ... LAUGHING.

> TOMMY CALLAHAN:
> *Hey John, Johnny. Look at me. I'm fuckin' flying, man. FLYING.*

Tommy LOCKS eyes on Johnny.

> TOMMY CALLAHAN:
> *Who says Port-a-Geese can't fly?*

Tommy takes a running lead and LEAPS off the roof as fireworks EXPLODE behind him.

115 EXT: JOHNNY'S APARTMENT BUILDING - LATE NEXT DAY

Grace sits on the apartment stoop, writing in her notebook. Her cell phone rings - Caller ID: Joey.

> JOHNNY :
> *What are you doing here?*

GRACE (looking up, ignoring Joey's call):
Waiting for you.

JOHNNY:
Everything okay?

GRACE:
I just heard about Tommy.

Johnny squats down next to her.

GRACE (taking his hand):
I'm so sorry, Johnny.

Johnny squeezes his little sister's hand.

JOHNNY:
You know ... Tommy was my first American friend. Everybody else treated me like dirt ...

Except for Tommy.

(holding back tears)

Shit, Grace. We were all there. Just watching. I did nothing. Nothing to stop him.

(raking his fingers through his hair)

I don't want to talk about it anymore.

They sit in silence as Grace fiddles with her ringless finger.

GRACE:
I saw Little Louie and Fat Manny coming out of the Tremont Lounge this morning. They were already totally wasted. I don't think they even knew who I was.

119

JOHNNY (unusually short with Grace):
Yeah. So. What's that got to do with me? I'm not their freaking babysitter.

GRACE:
I didn't say you were.

Grace cell phone rings ... Joey again. She silences her phone.

GRACE:
John, I'm not stupid. Just because we never talk about anything in this family, doesn't mean I don't know what's going on.

(pause)

I know what you all do.

Johnny stands up abruptly. Looks straight at Grace.

JOHNNY:
Yeah. That's right, Grace. I never snagged one of them fancy office jobs like Mr. Brady.

(a beat)

Do you really think when I was a little kid I dreamed of becoming a low-life loser scumbag?

GRACE (taken aback):
No. That's not what I meant. That's not who you are at all.

Grace grabs for his hand. He pulls away, turns away.

Johnny STARES down the street:

His old, dreaded school building is now converted to "Longfellow Luxury Living Condos." The sign covers the wall where Billy Maguire had spray-painted PORTAGEES SUCK!

JOHNNY (his back to Grace):
The first time I heard the word Portagee, I had no idea what it meant. I thought it was like, you know, when you call Tom - Tommy...just a nickname.

(a beat)

But I fucking learned to hate that word. And anyone who said it.

(turning to Grace)

All I ever wanted was to just fit in. You know? Be American.

Just a regular Joe.

He sits back down on the stoop next to Grace. Grabs her notebook, leafs through it.

JOHNNY:
You know Grace. I'm not smart like you. But on that street, I'm a real big deal. I ain't just another dumb Portagee. I'm Johnny FUCKING Vieira.

(a beat)

I got really good at hustling. But I never felt good about it.

116 INT. TREMONT BAR & LOUNGE - NIGHT

The dimly lit, smoke-filled bar is packed. Old drunks stagger out, hard-looking girls smoke cigarettes, chug beers.

An out-of-uniform Billy Maguire leans up against the bar nursing a beer ... peering over at Johnny and Fat Manny sharing a booth.

Johnny rubs the dark circles under his eyes - distraught, haunted with guilt over Tommy.

JOHNNY (to Manny):
That's it. I'm done. I'm fuckin' out of here.

FAT MANNY:
What are you nuts? We finally make it in and you wanna get out. That ain't what Tommy would want.

JOHNNY:
For Christ sakes Manny. We were all so fuckin' wasted. We laughed when he jumped...laughed.

FAT MANNY:
Johnny. Tommy was a wild man. You know all that shit was gonna catch up to him. His luck just ran out.

Johnny SLAMS his fist on the table. Maguire turns around.

JOHNNY:
That's just it, Manny. We've been lucky too long. And I'm just sick and tired of pretending the shit we're doing ain't wrong.

(a beat)

Between Tommy and that little Souza kid...

FAT MANNY (interrupting):
None of that was your fault. You wasn't the one sellin' the Souza kid drugs.

JOHNNY:
Manny, he was FUCKING 12 years old.

FAT MANNY (callously):
Tough shit. People OD every day. Anyways, where you gonna make that kind of money?

(laughing)

122

> *You gonna get yourself a real job? Flipping burgers at Burger King?*

(downing his beer)

> *And what? You think O'Leary's gonna let you just walk away.*

> JOHNNY:
> *I KNOW how to keep my mouth shut. O'Leary knows that.*

CLOSE VIEW ON: Billy Maguire, downing his beer, his eyes BORE into Johnny. He pulls out his phone, walks out of the bar.

CUT TO:

117 INT. FATIMA'S AND EDDIE'S BEDROOM - MORNING

In his underwear, Eddie is rummaging through drawers - yanking things out, making a mess.

Wearing her bathrobe, Fatima walks in.

> EDDIE (yelling):
> *Where the hell are my cut-offs?*

He pulls out her new red bathing suit.

> EDDIE (holding it up):
> *What the hell is this?*

> FATIMA:
> *It's nothin.' It's just a bathing suit. I thought ... maybe, I could wear something pretty. You know, for a change.*

Eddie gets aggressively closer to Fatima.

EDDIE:
Don't be STUPID.

Holding the bathing suit, he heads towards the kitchen.

118 INT. KITCHEN

He opens up a drawer, pulls out a scissors.

EDDIE:
Here's what I think of your new look.

Eddie cuts up the bathing suit.

FATIMA:
Eddie, stop it. Please.

She grabs for the bathing suit, he HITS her hard with the back of his hand. She falls back. But this time - GETS UP, goes for his face. Scratches it deep.

Eddie drops the bathing suit and scissors.

EDDIE:
You bitch.

He grabs her throat, choking her.

A Child CRIES OUT:
MOMMY!

119 EXT. OUTSIDE OF FATIMA AND EDDIE'S APARTMENT - CONTINUOUS

Dressed for the beach, Grace rings the apartment door bell several times. NO answer.

Heads towards the back porch. Runs up two flights of stairs. Knocks on the back door. NO answer.

GRACE (pushing open the door):
Hey, it's me.

120 INT. KITCHEN

Sitting on the floor, playing with her little brother, Eddie - Linda is in her bathing suit, sporting swimming goggles.

GRACE:
Hey pumpkin, where's mommy?

Linda points towards the bedroom.

LITTLE LINDA:
We still going to the beach?

GRACE:
Yeah, sure we are.

Nearby an open scissors and slivers of the red bathing suit litter the floor. Grace picks up the scissors, heads towards the bedroom.

121 INT. BEDROOM

A still body lies in bed, covers pulled fully over head.

GRACE (concerned):
Fatima. You ok?

No answer. Walks closer.

GRACE:
Fatima. Querida. Honey. Are you alright?

Grace slowly pulls off the covers.

RECOILS. As her sister's matted hair and badly swollen face is revealed.

Grace gently touches Fatima's face.

> GRACE (crying):
> *Oh Fatima, I'm so sorry. This is all my fault.*
>
> FATIMA (softly):
> *It's not ... it's not your fault.*
>
> GRACE:
> *That's it! You're leaving. Right now.*
>
> FATIMA:
> *You don't understand.*
>
> GRACE (calmly):
> *No, you're right. I don't. I don't understand at all. That monster almost killed you.*

(pause)

> *How much more are you going to take?*

Fatima pulls the covers over her head ... sobs.

> GRACE:
> *I'm calling Johnny.*

122 *INT. FATIMA AND EDDIE'S KITCHEN - LATER*

Eddie, whistling, walks through the door, carrying a cooler.

> EDDIE (breezing in as if nothing happened):
> *Hey Fatima, I'm home. Guess what I have? Lobstas ... your favorite.*

SILENCE.

> EDDIE:
> *Fatima, you home?*

Stepping on the slivers of the red bathing suit, he enters the bedroom, carrying the cooler.

123 INT. BEDROOM

The bed is unmade. The closet door is wide open. Fatima's clothes are missing.

> EDDIE:
> *You Bitch!! You friggin' Bitch!*

He whips the cooler on the floor. The lid flips open. Water and lobsters spill out. The floor is filled with seaweed and lobsters crawling every which way.

124 INT. VIEIRA APARTMENT HALL INCESSANT DOORBELL RINGING - CONTINUOUS

Grace lifts the front door curtain. Eddie's ENRAGED FACE PRESSES UP AGAINST THE GLASS.

> GRACE:
> *Go AWAY Eddie. She's never going back to you.*

> EDDIE:
> *Open the friggin' door. She's my wife. This ain't got nothing to do with you.*

> GRACE:
> *She's MY sister. It has everything to do with me.*

125 INT. KITCHEN

Fatima and her crying kids huddle around the table.

DOOR BELL RINGS. RINGS. RINGS.

Fatima starts to get up.

Bella presses both hands down on Fatima's shoulders - NODDING TO HER - NO.

126 EXT. OUTSIDE DOOR

Eddie BANGS on the front door with his fists - HARD!

> EDDIE:
> *Grace, open the door. NOW! She's MY God damn wife.*
>
> GRACE:
> *Go to hell, Eddie. Get out of here or I'm calling the cops.*

Eddie KICKS the door.

> EDDIE:
> *Little bitch. You're just like your bitch sister.*

CUT TO:

127 EXT. PLUM ISLAND - A FEW DAYS LATER

Wooden lobster trap cages bob up and down along the coastline. Eddie, dressed in scuba gear, sits on the rocks transferring lobsters from a cage into a cooler.

He's drinking beer, tossing the crashed cans into the ocean.

> JOHNNY:
> *You got a permit for those lobsters?*

Johnny moves in closer to Eddie.

> EDDIE:
> *Who the hell are you? The lobsta' police?*
>
> JOHNNY:
> *Yeah, I guess you could say that.*

From behind his back, Johnny pulls out an aluminum baseball bat.

BAM! HITS Eddie right across the stomach, then rams it into his back.

Eddie is SCREAMING.

> JOHNNY (in a RAGE):
> *You think you're a big man beating up on women. The only reason you ain't a dead man Eddie is 'cause my sister loves those kids too much.*

Johnny raises his foot and VICIOUSLY kicks Eddie in the head.

128 INT. CATHOLIC CHURCH - CONTINUOUS

Fatima's black eye is covered up with make-up. She fusses with her bangs to cover up the bruise.

She's sitting in a church pew next to Grace and Bella - all holding open their book of scriptures, following along with the Mass.

An old, pasty-white priest dressed in elaborate vestments stands in front of an ornate altar. He places his hands on the pulpit, rising taller as he opens the bible.

His beady eyes peer through thin-framed glasses.

> PRIEST:
> *Genesis 3:16 ... Unto the woman I said I will greatly multiply thy sorrow and thy conception. In sorrow though shalt bring forth children and thy desire shall be thy husbands. And he shall rule over thee.*

Fatima bites her bottom lip as Grace SHUTS her book, tossing it onto the pew.

Embarrassed, Bella looks around nervously, hoping no one noticed Grace's book toss.

Grace reaches over, takes hold of her sister's hand.

CUT TO:

129 INT. DRY CLEANERS - CLOSING TIME, NEXT DAY

Grace is behind the counter. Joey, still in work clothes, stands opposite her. She's pointing her finger in his face.

The door BELL CHIMES. Alex, looking DAPPER, enters - carrying a bundle of shirts.

Grace stops talking. Joey raises his hands in a WHATEVER, 'I give up' fashion. Barges out the door, bumping into Alex.

>ALEX MCPHEARSON:
>*Are you okay?*

Grace nods yes.

Alex glances out the window as Joey gets in his car and speeds away.

>ALEX MCPHEARSON:
>*Who was that?*

>GRACE (flatly):
>*Nobody.*

130 EXT. DRY CLEANERS PARKING LOT

Still in the parking lot, Alex is shooting the breeze with Turtle.

Grace walks into the lot looking around.

>GRACE (to Turtle):
>*Where's Joey?*

>TURTLE:
>*I dunno. He was here a minute ago.*

GRACE:
Okay then. Bye. See you next week.

TURTLE (surprised):
Ain't you gonna wait for him?

GRACE:
Nope.

Grace waves goodbye.

TURTLE:
You wanna ride?

GRACE:
No thanks. I feel like walking.

Turtle shrugs his turtle-like shoulders. Alex gets into his car.

131 *EXT. BROADWAY LIQUORS*

From the outside of the small liquor store window, hangs a big poster: Massachusetts 'A Dollar & A Dream' Lottery ... "Play & Win Millions Today."

Joey sits in his car, his hands clenching the steering wheel. He stares at the sign the same way a junkie longs for crack.

132 *EXT. A BLOCK FROM THE DRY CLEANERS*

From his car, Alex spots Grace walking and pulls up beside her.

ALEX MCPHEARSON:
Hey, hop in. I'll give you a ride.

GRACE:
Thanks, I'm fine.

Leaning over the passenger's seat, Alex swings open the car door.

ALEX MCPHEARSON:
Come on. It's just a ride.

Grace hesitates ... gets in.

133 INT. ALEX'S CAR

ALEX MCPHEARSON:
Grace. I'm really, really sorry. I had no idea.

GRACE:
You stand up there teaching all these high and mighty moral lessons. And yet, you still judged me. Why ... Because I work in a dry cleaners?

ALEX MCPHEARSON:
I have no excuse. I fell right into the trap. I'm a big fat elitist jerk.

GRACE:
Clearly ... Maybe you should think about teaching a different kind of class.

Grace folds her arms, turns her face away and stares straight out the car window.

AWKWARD SILENCE.

ALEX MCPHEARSON (trying to lighten the mood):
So, how did you end up at Tufts?

GRACE:
Scholarship. I'm the first. The first to graduate from high school. Go to college. You know, your "American Dream" poster child.

ALEX MCPHEARSON (playfully nudging her elbow):
Clearly.

(a beat)

> *Listen. Maybe I can make things up to you.*

Grace shoots him an uncertain 'Like how?' look.

> ALEX MCPHEARSON:
> *Let's go grab a coffee.*

> GRACE:
> *I thought this was just a ride.*

> ALEX MCPHEARSON:
> *Okay, then. We'll get it to go.*

Grace finally smiles, giving in.

134 INT. NEIGHBORHOOD DUNKIN' DONUTS

All the Portuguese locals STARE as Grace stands at the counter with tall, blonde Alex.

> GRACE:
> *Hi, Senhora Medeiros. Two regulars please.*

Senhora Medeiros gives an UNSUBTLE head nod towards Alex.

> SENHORA MEDEIROS (in Portuguese):
> *Who is this man?*

> GRACE (in Portuguese):
> *My professor. From school.*

With a DISAPPROVING look, Senhora Medeiros hands Grace the coffees and waves away Alex's money. He places the money in the tip jar.

With every eyeball on them, Alex and Grace walk over and sit at a corner table.

ALEX MCPHEARSON:
So this is your neighborhood?

GRACE:
Yep. These are my people.

Looks over at Senhora Medeiros.

That's Joey's aunt.

Senhora Medeiros GLARES over - all old world nosey, up in your business... She picks up the phone. DIALS.

ALEX:
Joey. The boyfriend?

Grace rolls her thumb around her naked ring finger.

ALEX:
So what were you two fighting about?

GRACE:
Things.

Wanting to change the subject - Grace smiles across the room - EYES each one of her nosey neighbors ... one by one.

GRACE (proudly describes her tribe to Alex):
They all came here with nothing. That's Senhor Cabral. He now owns the fish market. Over there is Maria, she runs the beauty shop. Turtle - you know. And Senhora Medeiros. She and her husband own TEN Dunkin' Donuts. They're loaded. But every day, she still comes in here and works that counter.

ALEX MCPHEARSON:
Sounds like they figured out how to buy themselves their own boat.

Grace shoots him a 'Wow. You were actually listening' look.

> ALEX MCPHEARSON:
> *I gather your plan is to one day own one of those boats.*

(drawing with his hand in the air)

> *The Grace Vieira. Attorney at Law.*

> GRACE (laughing):
> *Yep. A whole fleet of them.*

Grace folds her napkin into tiny squares.

> GRACE:
> *You know. I really am serious about law school ...*

(laughing)

> *Just gonna need one HECK of a bake sale to pay for it.*

> ALEX MCPHEARSON (charmed by her):
> *Your parents must be really proud of you.*

Grace folds and refolds the napkin even smaller.

> GRACE:
> *My mom is.*

(shredding the napkin into pieces)

> *My dad. He... He died.*

(a beat)

> *I was just a baby.*

Alex reaches over for Grace's hand.

An animated Senhora Medeiros points over to Grace and Alex.

Joey stomps over to their table. Alex removes his hand from Grace's.

> JOEY (Looking at Alex, but addressing Grace):
> *Why didn't you wait for me?*
>
> GRACE (pissed):
> *And, why did you just take off on me? Where'd you go in such a rush, Joey?*

Joey shoves his hands into his pants pockets - stuffing in a wad of lottery tickets.

> JOEY:
> *SCREW you, Grace. You're not my mother.*

Joey stomps out.

> ALEX MCPHEARSON:
> *What was that all about?*

Grace looks out the window as Joey passes by - pulling out a Lottery Scratch Ticket from his pocket.

135 INT. BELLA'S SEWING ROOM - LATER THAT NIGHT

A small overhead lamp shines down on Grace lying down on the daybed reading the book from her assignment: "The Hidden Injuries of Class and Religion."

CLOSE ON: Napoleon Bonaparte quote:

"*Religion is what keeps the poor from murdering the rich.*"

Phone RINGS.

> BELLA:
> *Grace, is Joey.*

GRACE:
I don't want to talk to him.

Bella enters the doorway of the sewing room.

BELLA:
Why? What he do?

Grace stares down at her book.

Bella sits on the edge of the day bed, raises Grace's chin up, examining her face.

BELLA (tenderly):
Tell me querida. Did he hit you?

Grace nods, No.

BELLA:
He find a new girl?

GRACE:
No.

BELLA:
Then what? What can be so bad?

GRACE (blurts out):
I don't want to be with Joey anymore.

BELLA:
But why? Joey's like family.

GRACE:
He's gambling, Ma. Just throwing his money away.

BELLA:
Oh... that's nothing. I talk with his Mama. We make him stop.

GRACE:
It's not just that ...

BELLA:
Is gonna be okay. I go get you some nice soup, it make you feel better.

Slamming her book shut.

GRACE:
I don't want any stupid soup, Ma. I don't want Joey. And I don't want to get married. I want my own life. My own money. My own apartment.

BELLA (annoyed):
Não sejas túla. Only PUTAS live by themselves in apartments. God NO likes.

GRACE:
Oh yeah Ma, what if God doesn't know everything? What if God isn't such a nice guy after all?

BELLA (incensed, in Portuguese):
Grace Isabel Vieira, I raised you better than that.

(English)

God is good. God no hurt nobody.

GRACE:
Really? What about Fatima? Is that what God's goodness looks like?

BELLA (adamant):
Is NOT God's fault.

GRACE (tearing up):
Mommy, I just don't love Joey that way.

BELLA:
No woman loves a man when she first marries him. That comes later when you have babies. You gonna see.

Bella gets up to leave.

BELLA:
Joey is a good Portuguese boy. And you gonna be a good girl for God.

Bella ROUGHLY slides the doorway curtain SHUT.

Grace FLINGS her book across the room.

136 INT. VIEIRA FAMILY KITCHEN - NEXT DAY

Grace and Fatima, her face still bruised, are unloading bags of groceries on the counter.

FATIMA (to Grace):
Mario called. He said Johnny put Eddie in the hospital.

Grace continues sorting through bags - not responding.

FATIMA:
I thought he was just gonna scare him a little. You know, have a talk ... I kinda feel bad.

GRACE (reeling around):
You feel what? Are you nuts? The guy's a pyscho animal. Don't even tell me you're thinking about going back to him.

FATIMA:
I told you, he's not like that all the time.

GRACE:
All the time? For God sakes, Fatima. He almost killed you. Don't be STUPID!

ANGRY, Fatima SLAPS Grace.

> FATIMA:
> *Don't you ever call me STUPID.*

(pointing her finger at Grace)

> *You think it's so easy, don't you? You've got it made. Everybody loves Grace.*

Grace's FROZEN. Holding her hand against her red, stinging face.

> FATIMA (mimicking):
> *Grace is special, Grace is the smart one. She's different...Grace is going places.*
>
> *Well, I wanted to go places too.*

(pounding her chest)

> *I was something special, too.*

(a beat)

> *I never wanted to come to this stupid country. NEVER. You know nothing about how hard it was for us... for me. You know nothing about me. You have no idea what it's like to have my life... To feel my shame.*

Fatima sits, puts her head down on the table and weeps.

> GRACE:
> *Fatima, I'm so sorry.*
>
> FATIMA:
> *You just don't understand. We left everything behind. We had nothing. No friends, no money. We were so poor. Can't you see ... Eddie Pacheco thought I was beautiful. HE made me feel special.*

137 INT. BELLA'S SEWING ROOM

Grace checks in on Fatima. She's curled-up, sleeping on the daybed facing the wall. Grace gently touches her sister's hair. Not turning around, Fatima speaks facing the wall.

> FATIMA:
> *I'm sorry, querida. I didn't mean those things.*
>
> GRACE:
> *I know.*
>
> FATIMA:
> *It's not that you dream too big.*

(tears rushing her eyes)

> *It's just that I forgot how.*

138 INT. VIEIRA FAMILY KITCHEN - A FEW DAYS LATER

Holding a huge bouquet of flowers, Eddie's kneeling in front of a sobbing Fatima.

> FATIMA:
> *No, Eddie. I won't. I'm not gonna live like that anymore.*

Grace enters.

Eddie, his arm in a sling, hovers over Fatima.

> GRACE:
> *What are you doing here?*

Eddie turns, his face is seriously bruised with an ugly row of stitches above his left eye. Ignoring Grace, he turns back to Fatima.

EDDIE:
Fatima, please, I swear to God. It'll be different this time.

GRACE:
Eddie, get out of my house. She's not going back to you.

EDDIE (pleading to Fatima):
Fatima, please. I promise I can change. Just give me one more chance.

GRACE (pleading):
Fatima, he'll never change. Please don't go back to that house.

Eddie takes Fatima by the arm, leading her out of the kitchen. Grace grabs for her sister's hand. Fatima takes Grace's hand, kisses it.

FATIMA (giving in, tearful):
I have to go Grace. Keeping your family together always comes first, right? Isn't that what Ma always says. And the church. Right?

139 INT. TUFTS UNIVERSITY AUDITORIUM - DAY

Grace slips into her self-designated last row seat near the EXIT sign.

Professor McPhearson is standing in front of the big white board, behind him scrawled in big capital letters:

FATALISM VS. DESTINY

ALEX MCPHEARSON:
The Epic Battle of the Ages. Fate versus Destiny. If our lives are really predetermined, what role do we have, what say - if any? Where do we end up? And with whom? Who really chooses?

Is it Destiny or Fate?

And what's the difference?

(he turns to write on the board in big letters)

FREE WILL! CHOICE!

Grace is feverishly taking notes, capturing every word.

> ALEX MCPHEARSON:
> *Destiny is your place in life.*

(pacing the floor)

> *Where you're born. Who your parents are. Your place in society. But it does not dictate that where you start is where you'll end up. Because we all have the power of free will.*

ALEX LOCKS EYES ON GRACE ...

FLASHING before Grace: The image of Fatima, her face bruised, walking out of the kitchen, going back to Eddie.

> ALEX MCPHEARSON:
> *Fatalism, on the other hand, is the Death Star of Destiny. Fatalists believe your whole life is predetermined. There is no free will. You are ... forgive my French ...*

(scribbles on the board)

SCREWED!

(class chuckles)

> *Which we know is not true. Because as human beings we have the ability to Think. Take Action. Choose.*
>
> *Why else would you all be sitting here right now?*

Class laughs.

> ALEX MCPHEARSON:
> *Okay. Final paper due in on Tuesday. And no. You do not have a choice.*

Students scurry out as Grace lingers in the back packing up her things.

Alex HURRIES up the steps towards Grace.

> ALEX MCPHEARSON:
> *Could you sit any further back?*
>
> GRACE (smiles):
> *Makes for a quick getaway.*

He hands her a business card.

> GRACE:
> *What's this?*
>
> ALEX MCPHEARSON:
> *My way of making it up to you.*

She looks at the card confused. Then looks back at him.

> ALEX MCPHEARSON:
> *It's my friend's company. They're hiring. They'll be on campus next week interviewing graduating seniors. You're scheduled for noon on Wednesday.*

Grace's stares down at the card:
'Robert Winn, President. APA Foreign Language Recruiters'

> ALEX MCPHEARSON (with a wink):
> *Maybe jumpstart that "bake sale" of yours.*

Grace, looking down, rolls the card between her fingers ... not wanting to tear up.

> GRACE:
> *Maybe, you're not such a jerk, after all.*

Not expecting it - Grace lays a big Portuguese hug on Alex.

Liking it, Alex hugs her back, tight.

140 INT. VIEIRA KITCHEN, AFTER GRADUATION - MIDNIGHT

The kitchen is dark except for the dim light glowing from the TICKING 'Last Super' clock.

Carrying her graduation gown over her arm, Grace tosses it over the chair.

Johnny speaks up softly from across the room.

> JOHNNY:
> *Hey.*
>
> GRACE (startled):
> *What are you doing here?*
>
> JOHNNY:
> *Waiting for you.*

Grace opens the refrigerator door. Stands there, staring in.

> JOHNNY:
> *You made us all really proud today.*

Shuts the fridge and sits next to Johnny in the darkness.

> JOHNNY:
> *Imagine us. All sitting there, right next to them doctors and lawyers, while my little sister goes up to get the exact same diploma all them rich kids were getting.*

Grace leans her head down on the table.

JOHNNY:
What's the matter? This should be the best day of your life.

GRACE:
It's not. Ma's all mad at me ... Everything's just a mess.

JOHNNY (interrupting):
Ah come on Grace. I love Ma. But she's been the patron saint of guilt ever since I can remember.

GRACE:
Yeah, but ...

JOHNNY:
Yeah but nothin.' Anyway, Ma's not your problem. Joey is.

Johnny holds her tenderly by the shoulders.

JOHNNY:
Baby Girl, you've always been way too top-shelf for that kid. You need to dump his sorry ass, right now.

GRACE:
What about Ma? She loves Joey. She'll never forgive me if I leave him.

JOHNNY:
For Christ's sake Grace. I thought college was suppose to make you smarter.

Johnny gets up - unintentionally knocking over the chair, dropping Grace's graduation gown to the floor.

JOHNNY (getting angry):
Ma made me. Ma wouldn't let me. It's God. It's the Devil. The only luck we have is bad luck.

(slowly)

I am so SICK of this family's sea of excuses.

Grace's STUNNED ... NOT A SIDE OF JOHNNY SHE KNOWS.

> JOHNNY:
> *Shit Grace, I've been using them excuses all my life.*

(a beat)

> *I just don't want you to!*

He pulls up the chair, takes hold of both her hands.

> JOHNNY:
> *Listen to me, Baby Girl.*
>
> *We can't change nobody. Look at Tommy. Fatima.*
>
> *The life you pick is the life you're gonna live. You can make it good. Or one fucking hell ... But NOBODY can choose for you. Not Ma. Not God. Not nobody.*

Johnny kisses the top of her forehead.

> JOHNNY:
> *Every choice has a consequence and we own every single one of them.*

Johnny gets up to leave, turning on the overhead light.

In his hand, he's holding up Grace's MISSING PROMISE RING.

> JOHNNY:
> *Joey pawned it. For gambling money.*

Johnny places the ring on the table, slides it towards Grace.

> JOHNNY:
> *You just can't fix broken people.*

Grace's mouth just drops.

141 INT. EDDIE AND FATIMA'S KITCHEN - NEXT MORNING

Drizzly, hot summer day.

Thunder CRACKLES in the background. Eggs sizzle in the frying pan as Fatima cracks them open into the hot oil.

Little Eddie sits at the table coloring.

Drinking a beer, Eddie's standing in front of the open refrigerator.

> EDDIE:
> *There's nothin' ever good to eat in this friggin' house.*
>
> FATIMA (looking up from chopping):
> *Eddie, what are you talking about, there's a ton of stuff in there.*

Disgusted, he shuts the refrigerator door, turns and stubs his toe on a toy truck.

> EDDIE (turning to Little Eddie):
> *SHIT! How many times have I told you. Put your friggin' toys away?*

Eddie GRABS the toy truck and HURLS it out the window, glass SPLATTERS all over the kitchen.

Little Eddie CRIES and runs over to his mother.

> FATIMA:
> *Eddie, what the hell is wrong with you?*
>
> EDDIE:
> *Stop crying you little sissy mama's boy.*

Eddie pulls off his belt and heads towards Little Eddie. Fatima shields the child with her body.

FATIMA:
Eddie, stop it. How could you say those things to your own son?

EDDIE (mockingly):
So you say ...

Fatima maneuvers the child away from Eddie. Shoos him out of the kitchen.

FATIMA (to Little Eddie):
GO. Go play, baby.

EDDIE:
Yeah that's right "BABY" go play with your sissy ass dolls.

Little Eddie runs out.

Fatima grabs for the telephone, reaches for the receiver.

EDDIE:
Oh! What are you gonna do? Call your pussy ass brother?

CLOSE VIEW ON: Fatima's hand on the phone as Eddie WHIPS the phone out of her hand.

Fatima turns to him in RAGE. Grabs the HOT frying pan from the stove, WHIPS it at Eddie. The pan hits him HARD on the shoulder. He howls in pain.

She makes a run for the door. He grabs her back in by the hair, flinging her to the floor.

Eddie straddles a squirming Fatima, wrestling to get free. He rolls up his fist.

EDDIE:
You dumb ass Portagee. Coming after me like that. You'd still be cleaning toilets if it wasn't for me.

DISSOLVE TO BLACK:

Sounds of PUNCHING, SCREAMING ... Then Silence.

142   INT. JOEY'S APARTMENT - CONTINUOUS

Wearing a Tufts sweatshirt, Grace sits on the sofa, hugging her curled up legs - EYES FIXED on Joey.

He's clicking through the TV channels.

JOEY (stops on a Red Sox game):
Oh great. The game's still on.

Grace silently observes Joey as he interacts with the game.

JOEY:
Ah! Come on. Play the F-in' game.

GRACE:
How much you bet on the game?

Joey still talking to the television.

JOEY:
AAHHHH, no. You idiot.

GRACE:
Joey, did you hear me?

JOEY:
No. What?

GRACE:
It's over.

JOEY:
What? It's just the seventh inning.

GRACE:
Not the game, Joey ... Us. You. Me. We're done.

JOEY:
Why? I told you I ain't gamblin' no more.

Grace gets up, grabs the clicker, turns off the television. Joey grabs the clicker out of her hand ... about to turn the TV back on.

GRACE:
Johnny found my ring.

HOLY CRAP MOMENT ... Joey drops the clicker.

JOEY:
Grace, I swear to God, I was gonna get it back.

GRACE:
STOP IT, Joey! Just stop lying to me.

JOEY:
Come on Grace. You're making a big deal out of nothin'.

GRACE:
It's over, Joey.

(not sugarcoating it)

I'm moving to D.C.

JOEY:
D.C.? What the hell's in D.C.?

GRACE:
A job. I got a job as a translator at the Portuguese Embassy.

Grace heads towards the door. Joey moves in closer.

> JOEY:
> *So what? Now you're better than me cuz you went to fuckin' college. Leaving me for some dumb ass D.C. job.*

> GRACE:
> *That has nothing to do with it and you know it.*

Grace grabs for the door knob. Joey BLOCKS her way.

> JOEY:
> *I can't believe your Ma is good with all this.*

RADIO SILENCE FROM GRACE.

> JOEY:
> *You haven't told her, have you?*

(laughing at her)

> *Your Ma's never gonna let you move to D.C.*

(a beat)

> GRACE:
> *Shut up, Joey. I'm not ten years old anymore.*

> JOEY:
> *You are to her.*

> GRACE:
> *You know, I've tried so hard to always be the good one. Not wanting to disappoint her or make her cry. But now, all that trying is just suffocating me. Just like you are.*

Grace digs into her jean's pocket and pulls out the ring ... HOLDS IT UP.

GRACE:
I don't like that version of me anymore.

She drops the ring, it PINGS off the glass coffee table and rolls onto the floor.

143 EXT. JOEY'S APARTMENT

CRYING, GRACE SLAMS the door shut, RUSHES up the street, crying.

CALLING and waving from across the street.

ALEX MCPHEARSON:
Grace. Hey Grace.

Grace turns as Alex McPhearson comes walking out of Cabral's Atomic Fish Market.

ALEX MCPHEARSON (holding up a paper bag):
'Uma libra.' I ordered in Portuguese.

Wiping at her eyes, Grace crosses the street walking straight towards a smiling Alex.

SIRENS BLARING. A POLICE CAR AND AMBULANCE WHIZ BETWEEN THEM.

Up the street, a blur of red and blue police lights FLASH outside of Fatima's apartment.

144 EXT. FATIMA AND EDDIE'S APARTMENT

Running towards the flashing lights, Grace pushes through a crowd of neighbors, gawking, muttering - all standing behind a yellow police tape:

POLICE LINE: DO NOT CROSS.

GRACE:
What's going on?

A neighbor recognizing Grace, BURSTS into tears.

Grace slides under the police tape. Bolts up the stairs. She's stopped by Officer Billy Maguire.

GRACE:
What happened? Where's my sister?

BILLY MAGUIRE (professional, but genuine):
I'm sorry Grace. She's gone.

GRACE:
Gone? Gone where?

He stands silent, looking away - not making eye contact.

Grasping the finality of his words - Grace is NUMB. FROZEN as her brain goes into a dizzying fog. Then, out comes an ear-piercing SCREAM.

GRACE:
NOOOOOOOOOOOOOOOOO!

She punches at Maguire, crying, yelling, shoving. He holds her back firmly but kindly as she collapses to the ground.

FADE TO BLACK:

145 *EXT. CATHOLIC CHURCH - DAY*

The WAILING sound of a woman, howling in pain and grief is heard over the CLANGING church bells.

A white covered casket is wheeled out the church door. Followed by the same pasty, beady-eyed priest who had given the painful Genesis 3:16 sermon before.

PRIEST (V.O.):
"Unto the woman I will greatly multiply thy sorrow..."

The sermon rings in Grace's head.

Groaning with grief, Bella - barely able to walk - is held up by Johnny and Fat Manny.

Grace - stoic, emotionless - holds Fatima's children's hands.

A large group of mourners follow the casket: Joey, Turtle, Mr. Cabral, Mr. Silva, Senhora Medeiros, Little Louie, Billy Maguire, O'Leary, Alex McPhearson ...

Close view on Grace: her stoic expression CRUMBLES as her sister's casket is loaded into the hearse.

As the hearse's door closes, we catch a glimpse of the coffin with a tiny bronze plaque engraved: Spring Hill Caskets.

BELLA (V.O. from earlier):
God NO hurt nobody.

146 INT. BELLA'S SEWING ROOM - LATER THAT NIGHT

The room is dark.

A sliver of light from the hallway illuminates Grace lying on the daybed, curled around her Dora the Explorer doll ... weeping.

Bella quietly slips in, sits on the edge of the bed, gently pulling Grace's head onto her lap ... stroking her daughter's hair.

GRACE:
Do you ever wish that we'd never come here?

Bella fidgets with Jose's Saint Michael medallion hanging from around her neck.

BELLA:
Yes, querida ... but we were no safe there.

(Portuguese)

Sometimes, I think that all that sadness just followed me here like a little ghost.

Grace buries her face into her mother's lap as Bella continues stroking her hair.

BELLA:
Your brother, he tells me about your new job.

OH NO ... NOT expecting to hear that from her, Grace raises her head. Hair sticking to her tear-stained face.

BELLA:
Why you don't tell me?

Grace sits up ramrod straight on the bed, facing away from Bella.

BELLA:
Why you want to go so far away from home, from me?

Grace shifts nervously, readjusting herself, facing her mom.

GRACE:
I'm not going. I'm not taking the job.

BELLA:
Porque? Why?

GRACE:
Because of you.

BELLA:
Me? Why for me?

GRACE (determined not to cry):
Because ... I ... I can't. How can I go and just leave you here all alone to take care of Fatima's kids? That's just not fair.

Bella slides Grace's hair away from her face, gently placing the strands of hair, one by one, behind each ear.

BELLA:
So, you would do all this for me. For your mama?

Her dreams crushed, Grace nods, YES - looks away from her mother, fighting back tears.

BELLA takes Grace's hands in hers and kisses them.

BELLA:
You are a good girl. You always make your mama so proud.

Bella turns Grace's face towards her.

BELLA:
Querida filha, life is no fair.

(Portuguese)

There's always going to be someone who has to carry the pain.

Locking eyes on Grace ...

BELLA:
But, this is not your pain to carry.

(a beat)

BELLA:
I want you to go.

The Fado music softly returns.

147 EXT. FATIMA'S GRAVE, CEMETERY - FEW DAYS LATER

A freshly dug grave, surrounded by white flowers.

Grace's hand sweeps in and slowly begins to form a heart in the dirt, carefully filling in the shape of the heart with her fingers. She palms the space next to the heart, leaving her hand print.

148 EXT: VIEIRA FIRST FLOOR PORCH – BRIGHT, SUNNY DAY

Johnny loads luggage into Grace's car trunk as Bella, weeping, SMOTHERS Grace's face with kisses.

> BELLA (tapping Grace's head with hers):
> *You are brave. And strong.*
>
> *And so stubborn like your papa.*

Bella removes Jose's Saint Michael's medallion from her neck and places it over Grace's head. Carefully draping it on her daughter's chest ... Bella tenderly kisses the medallion.

> BELLA (tearing up):
> *He would be so proud of you.*

149 INT. GRACE'S CAR

Grace adjusts the rearview mirror: Johnny, his arm around a TEARFUL Bella, waves goodbye.

She turns on the ignition, fastens her seatbelt. Resting next to her on the passenger seat - her Dora the Explorer doll.

Grace waves one last goodbye out the window, DRIVING AWAY from the same inner city street where we first met her.

> GRACE (V.O.):
> *In the end, I do believe we own every choice we make. But, do we really have free will? Or do our circumstances blur the lines ... coloring the choices we have? ... I don't know.*

(pause)

> *But the one thing I do know, is that my beautiful sister didn't choose to die.*

(a beat)

> *She just CHOSE TO STAY.*

Grace turns up the car radio - LEAVING Tremont Street behind.

New, more hopeful, UPBEAT MUSIC PLAYS.

MUSIC CONTINUES OVER A SLOW MOTION IMAGE of ten-year-old Grace TWIRLING around, wearing her blue satin robe and feathered angel wings - first slowly, then SPEEDING UP as she TWIRLS herself into a BLUR of white feathers ... FLYING.

EPILOGUE

I started my writing journey by taking Robert McKee's "Story Seminar" not once, but twice – in Boston and Miami.

Wow! I felt like I was watching a one-man stage show – totally overwhelmed by all the insightful information coming out of his smoky voice.

After taking the seminar for the second time, I mustered the courage to actually approach Mr. McKee and introduce myself. I told him that I wanted to write a story which would inspire girls and women to not be victims in their lives – to give them the strength and courage to leave abusive or bad relationships.

His response after taking a long drag of his cigarette, "Listen doll, just write a fucking great story – that's all you need to do."

Okay then – that's what I put my mind to and started writing "What Geese Can't Fly" also titled at different points: "Grace's Goodbye" and "Leaving Tremont Street."

Along the way, I began collaborating with my author husband, Eric, and my brother, Joe, who helped to revive so many family memories.

The story is inspired by my family – first generation Portuguese immigrants who came here, like so many others, to escape poverty, a socialist dictatorship, and to give their children a better life.

Which, for me, they did.

But my experience of coming to America at five years old was very different from my 10 to 16-year-old brother and sisters' experiences. Life in America was hell for them. Their painful early years caused my sister and brother to make some miserable choices – choices that I vowed I would never make! You see, when I was younger, I judged them for the decisions they made; but then, I came to understand that our circumstances and environment can shape the choices we make. My empathy for them grew and grew.

With a little creative license, this is our story. I really started writing it just for myself. Then, it turned into writing something that might help or inspire someone, who may be living in misery or feeling trapped, to change their life and not give up hope. And to realize, there is always a choice to be made - but that choice can only be made by you.

Thank you for letting me share our story.

— Emily Fagundo Haggman

Special Thanks

This story would not be possible without the help of our family and friends. Starting with my husband, **Eric Haggman**, who is the award winning author of **THE APOLOGY**, and my writing partner; my younger brother **Joe "Kicka" Fagundo** whose memories of our early years in America was like a magical recording of many things that I had forgotten; **Bob Hohman, Marianne Moloney, Billy Gersh, Kyle Peters** and **Eden Rubel**, our friends at **The Gersh Agency** who expertly guided us through the script writing and rewriting process and introduced us to Hollywood; **Melissa Cunha Roberts**, our niece and tireless assistant who helped manage the countless variations and rewrites; **Ann Messenger**, who designed the book and read and reread every version, offering insights; **Katie Pensak** who designed the cover; the many friends and family who read the story and gave me welcoming input:

Julia Platt Leonard, Linda Russo, May Kernan, Patti Melaragno, Connie and Gary Romagna, Jim Beardsworth, Alicia Crichton, Chris Engel, Mary Ingram-Schatz, Joe and Mary Ellen Amicone, Marit von Tetzcher, Joann Mackenzie, Tricia Castraberti, Matt Haggman, Danet Linares, Grace Leite, Odete Pascoa, Lynn and Nick Kimball, Michael Liston, Lynn Robinson, Steve Cowell, Jacquie Loughery, Brownell Landrum, Jerome Hill, Rishi Rajani, Jane Goldenring, Karen Lunder, and **Margaret French Isaac**.

And most of all our **Fagundo family**, who allowed us to take some creative liberties with not just my story, but theirs, too - encouraging the journey all the way: our beloved **Mary, Bella, John, Joe (Kicka), Gloria, Alan, Kiki, Gail, Kelly, Mike, Manuel, Joey, Joe, Melissa, Jagger, Jamie, Gianna, Mikey** and **Johnny** ...
love you too, too much.

Thank you all, *Emily*